## SUPER GENIUS
# PHYSICS QUIZ

An educationist by profession, **Vijaya Khandurie** has been writing on science for many years. A keen quiz and crossword enthusiast, he is also the honorary advisor to a bi-monthly magazine *Word Games & Puzzles*. Presently, he is working as an assistant director with the Directorate of Education, Delhi Government.

# SUPER GENIUS
# PHYSICS QUIZ

VIJAYA KHANDURIE

RUPA

Published by
Rupa Publications India Pvt. Ltd 2005
7/16, Ansari Road, Daryaganj
New Delhi 110002

*Sales centres:*

Allahabad Bengaluru Chennai
Hyderabad Jaipur Kathmandu
Kolkata Mumbai

ISBN: 978-81-291-0849-4

Fourth impression 2018

10 9 8 7 6 5 4

The moral right of the author has been asserted.

# CONTENTS

# PREFACE

## WHY THIS TITLE ?

In my forty years of experience as a lecturer in Physics and science educationist, I have witnessed a dramatic change in the awareness of school-going students, whether in the primary or senior classes. Some thirty years back, textbooks and some magazines were perhaps the only source of information and knowledge in science especially in India. Even in those days, our brilliant students secured admission in the IITs and other prestigious educational institutions. The competition was not tough, and on the basis of marks obtained in various educational boards, students were selected for higher studies.

With the IT boom, the scenario has completely changed. Now even a student of the 5th standard, especially one from a reputed Public School, can boast of throwing some light on quarks, genomes, etc. Their knowledge of these complex terms may be superficial, but at least they are aware of them. And, the main objective of quiz is after all to test one's awareness of things.

## WHO IS A GENIUS ?

A genius is one who has outstanding creative or intellectual ability. Here let us forget for the time being the 'creative' part. As per general standards, a person having an Intelligence Quotient (IQ) of 140 and above is considered to be a genius. IQ is related to intelligence. A person may be highly intelligent in the social field but lacking in other fields. A highly intelligent mathematician like Ramanujan may have a low profile in social affairs. IQ tests take note of verbal skills, numerical ability, logic, spatial discrimination, etc, but then there are many aspects which are ignored. Thus, often IQ tests fail to identify a genius. There is no dearth of examples where a person in his/her childhood was considered to be 'duffer', 'useless' but later was hailed as a genius (for example, Albert Einstein). Again, a person exerting a powerful influence on another, whether good or bad, is also a genius, e.g. Hitler.

But then this small book is not only for the 'genius' but anyone who thinks he/she is different from others. This book is meant for anyone who wants ot know about the nature and finer points of Physics.

As Alexander Pope, one of the greatest among English poets once said: 'Strength of mind is exercise not rest'. So young geniuses go ahead and get immersed in the vast ocean of Physics and enjoy!

## ACKNOWLEDGEMENTS

While compiling this book, I spent endless hours reading and enjoying a number of books on popular science. This small book is the by-product of that effort.

The great physicists who also happen to be great popular science writers are the main source of the sort of information and knowledge that has made this book.

I personally acknowledge my gratitude to the writers of the following books – *From Quark to Cosmos* (Leon Lederman), *Dreams of a Final Theory* (Steven Weinberg), *A Brief History of Time* (Stephen Hawking) and *The Nature of Time* (Thomas Gold). I think, anybody interested in Physics should read these books.

Apart from the above, I'm grateful to the American Centre and the British Library where I enjoyed reading the books.

Finally, I'm most grateful to my loving wife Manju Khandurie and my three loving daughters Ooshma, Oorja and Avritti.

# I

# PHYSICS IN THE PAST

1. Before 1729, when Pieter van Musschenbroek used the term 'Physics' for the first time, the subject was known as:
   (a) Science
   (b) Physical Science
   (c) Natural Science
   (d) Natural Philosophy

2. Who, in the year 1231, was the first to describe the science of optics?
   (a) Willebrord Snell
   (b) Giambattista Della Porta
   (c) Robert Grosseteste
   (d) John Pecham

3. The first volume of which famous treatise was published in the year 1686?
   (a) *Traite de la Lumiere* by C. Huygens
   (b) *Philosophiae Naturalis Principia Mathematica* by Isaac Newton
   (c) *On the Revolutions of the Heavenly Orbs* by N. Copernicus
   (d) *Traite de Dynamique* by Jean d'Alembert

4. In 1678, Christiaan Huygens explained the wave theory of light in his *Treatise on Light*, but this was published only in:
   (a) 1685            (b) 1690
   (c) 1705            (d) 1715

5. Who in 1808 discovered the polarisation of light and introduced the term 'polarisation'?
   (a) Thomas Young      (b) Christiaan Huygens
   (c) Etienne-Louis Malus    (d) David Brewster

6. Who was burnt to death for suggesting that the sun might be an ordinary star?
   (a) Giordano Bruno      (b) Galileo Galilei
   (c) Tycho Brahe        (d) Nicolaus Copernicus

7. Which of the following phenomena was not Galileo's observation?
   (a) Craters are present on the surface of the moon.
   (b) Planets move in elliptical orbits.
   (c) Jupiter is surrounded by four moons.
   (d) The phases Venus undergoes are similar to the phases of our moon.

8. The first scientist to apply scientific reasoning to cosmology was René Descartes. What was his theory called?
   (a) Tidal theory        (b) Nebular theory
   (c) Vortex theory       (d) Accumulation theory

9. *Hydrodynamica* explained Bernoulli's theorem in 1738. Who was the first to suggest this theorem?
   (a) Daniel Bernoulli     (b) Jacob Bernoulli
   (c) Johann Bernoulli     (d) Pierre Bernoulli

10. Who encouraged Newton to write his ideas for *Principia*?
    (a) Charles Du Fay          (b) John Canton
    (c) John Robinson           (d) Edmund Halley

11. In 1705, Francis Hanksbee conducted an important experiment in acoustics. The experiment dealt with:
    (a) vibrations in strings     (b) vibrations in air columns
    (c) a clock in vacuum
    (d) energy associated with sound

12. In 1672, a French scientist made an expedition to Cayenne to demonstrate that a pendulum of the same length has a longer time period on the equator than in France. Who was he?
    (a) René de Réaumur
    (b) Pieter van Musschenbroek
    (c) Jean Richer              (d) François Marie Arouet

13. Michael Faraday formulated the laws of electrolysis in 1833, but someone else introduced the terms electrode, anode, cathode, ion, anion, cation, and electrolyte. Who was that person?
    (a) John Daniell             (b) William Whewell
    (c) Heinrich Lenz            (d) G.P. Thomson

14. The year 1820 is famous for:
    I.   the discovery of electromagnetism by Oersted.
    II.  the formulation of basic laws of electromagnetism by Ampère.
    III. the construction of the first galvanometer by Schweigger.
    IV.  the discovery of the magnetic effect of electricity by Arago.

    Which of the following combinations is correct?
    (a) I and IV                 (b) II and IV
    (c) I, III, and IV           (d) I, II, III, and IV

15. Which remarkable Russian theorist described accurately the view of earth from an imaginary orbiting satellite?
    (a) H.G. Wells
    (b) Jules Verne
    (c) Konstantin Tsiolkovsky
    (d) Werner von Braun

16. In which year did Albert Einstein and Edward Morley conduct their famous experiment to verify the existence of ether?
    (a) 1881
    (b) 1884
    (c) 1887
    (d) 1889

17. 8 November 1895 is an important date in the history of Physics, because on this date:
    (a) J.J. Thomson discovered the electron.
    (b) W. Roentgen discovered X-rays.
    (c) the first issue of the *Physical Review* was published.
    (d) C.T.R. Wilson developed the cloud chamber.

18. Einstein's General Theory of Relativity created a stir in the scientific world. An expedition was organised to observe the 1919 solar eclipse and prove the theory. Who headed this famous expedition?
    (a) A.A. Michelson
    (b) Edward Morley
    (c) C. Gauillaume
    (d) Arthur Eddington

19. Who in 1939 suggested the name 'meson' for middle-weight particles?
    (a) Hideki Yukawa
    (b) Homi Bhabha
    (c) Abraham Pais
    (d) C. Anderson

20. 2 December 1942 is known for:
    (a) the creation of the first controlled chain reaction.
    (b) the activation of the first operational nuclear reactor.
    (c) the formulation of the Big Bang theory.
    (d) the development of the first thermonuclear device.

# CONTEMPLATION OF IDEAS

1. 'To believe the earth as the only populated world in infinite space is as senseless as to assert that on an extensive plane only one stalk of grain will grow.'
   Who contemplated this idea?
   (a) Metrodoros of Chios    (b) Eudoxus of Cnidus
   (c) Pappus of Alexandria (d) Regiomontanus

2. Which Austrian physicist developed the philosophy that all knowledge is simply sensation?
   (a) Rudolph Claussius    (b) Ernest Mach
   (c) Joseph Stephan      (d) Gustaf Kirchhoff

3. 'A pivoted magnetic needle placed parallel to a wire carrying an electric current makes oscillation.' Who among the following was the first to think about it?
   (a) André Marie Ampére    (b) Georg Simon Ohm
   (c) Hans Christiaan Oersted (d) Michael Faraday

4. Of the following physicists, who was the first to give the idea: 'Each pure substance has its own characteristic spectrum.'?
   (a) Gustav Kirchhoff      (b) William Hyde Wollaston
   (c) Robert Bunsen       (d) Joseph von Fraunhofer

5. Who, among the following, was the first to think: 'The light in proceeding from point to point travels along the route which minimises the time required.'?
   (a) Gottfried Leibnitz      (b) Christian Johann Doppler
   (c) Konrad Lorentz          (d) Pierre de Fermat

6. Of the following physicists, who formulated the concept, 'An increasing magnetic field creates an electric field, which grows and by its changing, generates a second magnetic field, which helps the first to crumble. The crumbling magnetic field in turn creates a new electric field in the opposite direction. These waxing and waning fields propagate through space.'?
   (a) Heinrich Hertz          (b) James Clerk Maxwell
   (c) Guglielmo Marconi       (d) Michael Faraday

7. 'If radiation could be increased, developed, and controlled, it would be possible to signal across space for considerable distances.' Who was the first to suggest this idea?
   (a) Alexander Graham Bell  (b) Lee de Forest
   (c) Guglielmo Marconi       (d) Heinrich Hertz

8. Who was the first to suggest this idea: 'Radiant energy can be emitted and absorbed by atoms only in discrete amount, called *quanta*.'?
   (a) Albert Einstein         (b) Max Planck
   (c) Niels Bohr              (d) Jules Henry Poincare

9. Name the physicist who formulated this idea: 'It is impossible to measure precisely the position and the velocity of an object simultaneously.'
   (a) P.A.M. Dirac            (b) Erwin Shroedinger
   (c) Max Born                (d) Karl Werner Heisenberg

10. Rejecting the orbiting h-electron idea and introducing the concept of cloud of probability and quantum theory was the brainchild of which physicist?
    (a) Max Born        (b) S.N. Bose
    (c) P.A.M. Dirac     (d) Enrico Fermi

11. Who was the first to propose this idea: 'A force that deflects alpha particles as much as 180 degrees must be electrical in nature and can be generated only if all the mass of the atom in concentrated in a minute central core, called the *nucleus*.'?
    (a) J.J. Thomson    (b) Ernest Rutherford
    (c) Niels Bohr       (d) Henry Moseley

12. The idea that 'a moving rod contracts in the direction of its motion' was formulated by which physicist?
    (a) Albert Einstein   (b) Hendrick Antoon Lorentz
    (c) George Francis Fitzgerald
    (d) Lorentz and Fitzgerald independently

13. 'Matter directs the space–time how to curve, and the curved space–time directs matter how to behave.' This was the central idea behind:
    (a) the special theory of relativity
    (b) the general theory of relativity
    (c) the big bang cosmology
    (d) the Lorentz–Fitzgerald contraction

14. 'No two electrons in an atom have all the four quantum numbers the same' is the concept behind which physical principle?
    (a) Pauli's exclusion principle
    (b) Heisenberg's uncertainty principle
    (c) Einstein's mass–energy equivalence
    (d) Principle of coincidence

15. 'A symmetry between matter and anti-matter is fundamental to cosmology, and hence if there is a galaxy, the anti-galaxy also exists.' This was the chief idea behind:
    (a) the Alfvén–Klein cosmology
    (b) the Hubble expansion
    (c) the Big Bang theory
    (d) the presence of black holes in the universe

16. Who commented: 'There is no escape from the conclusion that we are dealing with particles that are far far lighter than atoms'?
    (a) Rutherford, after discovering the nucleus
    (b) Bacquerel, after discovering radioactivity
    (c) Thomson, after discovering the electron
    (d) Einstein, after proposing the concept of photons

17. Who, in 1829, was the first scientist to suggest that the spectral line should be used as a standard of length?
    (a) Etienne–Louis Malus
    (b) Jacques Babinet
    (c) Thomas Young
    (d) Gustave–Gaspard Coriolis

18. 'If the source of sound moves towards the observer, the wavelength is compressed to a smaller length. If, on the other hand, the source is moving away from the observer the wavelength is stretched.' This idea was put forward for the first time by which physicist?
    (a) Nicolas Appert
    (b) Gottlieb Daimler
    (c) Christian Johann Doppler
    (d) Edwin Hubble

19. Glashow and Bjorken in 1964 thought about the symmetry between quarks and leptons and proposed a fourth quark. The idea was so charming that they called the new quark:
    (a) charm                    (b) strange
    (c) beauty                   (d) truth

20. Wilhelm Carl Werner Otto Fritz Franz Wien—quite a long name!—was awarded the Nobel Prize in 1911. Which idea did he formulate?
    (a) The total amount of energy of all wavelengths emitted by a black body varies with temperature.
    (b) The wavelength of radiation emitted from black bodies varies with temperature.
    (c) The intensity of radiation emitted from a black body varies with temperature.
    (d) The product of frequency and temperature of the radiation emitted by a black body is constant.

# 3

# MEASUREMENTS AND PHYSICAL UNITS

1. 'Ohm' is not the unit of which of the following physical quantities?
   (a) Reluctance
   (b) Reactance
   (c) Resistance
   (d) Impedance

2. Which of the following physical quantities has the same dimensional formula as momentum?
   (a) Force
   (b) Pressure
   (c) Impulse
   (d) Angular momentum

3. The dimensional formula for energy is:
   (a) $MLT^{-1}$
   (b) $ML^2 T^{-2}$
   (c) $ML^{-1}T^{-2}$
   (d) $MLT^{-2}$

4. What is the S.I. unit of magnetic field strength?
   (a) Gilbert
   (b) Oersted
   (c) Gauss
   (d) Ampère per metre

5. Which of the following does not represent the unit of mutual conductance?
   (a) Siemens
   (b) Mho
   (c) $Ohm^{-1}$
   (d) Ohm/m

6. Which of the following pairs does not have the same dimension?
   (a) impulse; linear momentum
   (b) force; surface tension
   (c) stress; pressure
   (d) frequency; angular velocity

7. 'Becquerel' is the unit to measure
   (a) activity of a radionuclide
   (b) absorbed dose
   (c) illuminance
   (d) specific energy imparted

8. What is the unit of magnetic flux density?
   (a) Weber                (b) Maxwell
   (c) Tesla                (d) Siemens

9. What is the cgs unit of viscosity?
   (a) Poise                (b) Stokes
   (c) Slug
   (d) Newton per metre square

10. 'Nit' is the unit of what?
    (a) Luminance           (b) Illumination
    (c) Luminous flux       (d) Luminous energy

11. What is the unit of acoustic absorption?
    (a) Sone                (b) Phon
    (c) Skot                (d) Sabin

12. What is the reciprocal of the impedance of an electric current?
    (a) Conductance         (b) Susceptance
    (c) Admittance          (d) Reactance

13. $ML^2 T^{-3}$ is the dimensional formula for which physical quantity?
    (a) work
    (b) power
    (c) stress
    (d) torque

14. A logarithmic unit expressing the ratio of power, voltage, current, or sound intensity is known as:
    (a) neper
    (b) bel
    (c) noy
    (d) nox

15. 'Gal', a measure of acceleration due to gravity, is equal to:
    (a) $1 \text{ nm/s}^2$
    (b) $1 \text{ mm/s}^2$
    (c) $1 \text{ cm/s}^2$
    (d) $1 \text{ m/s}^2$

16. Barn is a unit of area for measuring the cross-section of nuclei. It is equivilant to:
    (a) $10^{-24} \text{ mm}^2$
    (b) $10^{-24} \text{ cm}^2$
    (c) $10^{-24} \text{ dm}^2$
    (d) $10^{-24} \text{ m}^2$

17. The S.I. unit of dose equivalent is:
    (a) becquerel
    (b) curie
    (c) gray
    (d) sievert

18. Which of the following units is not used in the area of ionising radiation?
    (a) neper
    (b) rem
    (c) rad
    (d) roentgen

19. A measure of contrast in image reproduction is called:
    (a) phot
    (b) rad
    (c) gamma
    (d) talbot

13

20. What is the name of the unit, equal to $10^{-26}$ Wm$^{-2}$ Hz$^{-1}$ sr$^{-1}$ to measure the power received at the telescope from a cosmic radio source?

(a) erlang
(b) watt
(c) jansky
(d) lambert

# 4

# FROM ALPHA TO OMEGA

1. One peta-hertz is equal to:
   (a) $10^9$ Hz
   (b) $10^{12}$ Hz
   (c) $10^{15}$ Hz
   (d) $10^{18}$ Hz

2. The factor 0.000 000 000 000 001 is denoted by:
   (a) hecto
   (b) atto
   (c) pico
   (d) femto

3. The constant represented by 'K' and possessing numerical value of $1.3807 \times 10^{-23}$ joules/kelvin is called:
   (a) dielectric constant
   (b) Compton wavelength of the electron
   (c) Boltzmann constant
   (d) Stefan–Boltzmann constant

4. The symbol 'G' represents:
   I. Mutual conductance
   II. Gibbs function
   III. Gravitational constant

   Which combination is correct?
   (a) III only
   (b) I and III only
   (c) II and III only
   (d) I, II and III

5. Which of the following physical quantities is not represented by the Greek alphabet 'φ'?
   (a) Phase angle          (b) Luminous flux
   (c) Work function        (d) Magnetic flux

6. An atomic constant describing binding energy between an electron and the atomic nucleus is called:
   (a) Planck constant, h
   (b) Avogadro constant, L
   (c) Rydberg constant, R
   (d) Decay constant, $\lambda$

7. Dirac's constant, equal to h/2 $\pi$, is denoted by:
   (a) D                    (b) $\hbar$
   (c) $\Delta$             (d) H

8. What does the symbol '$g_m$' represent?
   (a) Milligram
   (b) Acceleration due to gravity
   (c) Transconductance
   (d) Free muon g-factor

9. The 'A', 'B' and 'C' bands of a carbon resistor have yellow, white and orange colours, respectively. This is equivalent to:
   (a) 39,000 ohms          (b) 49,000 ohms
   (c) 94,000 ohms          (d) 43,000 ohms

10. The numbers 2, 8, 20, 28, 50, 82, and 128, representing the number of protons in a nucleus are called:
    (a) Raynolds' numbers
    (b) Mach numbers
    (c) Loschmidt's numbers
    (d) Magic numbers

11. What does the set of letters O, B, A, F, G, K, M, R, N, S represent?
    (a) Fraunhofer's lines of the solar system
    (b) Classification of stars according to their surface temperatures
    (c) Sub-shells of atoms
    (d) Notations of diatonic scale

12. What does the symbol 'sr' represent?
    (a) Specific radioactivity     (b) Strontium
    (c) Steradian                  (d) Electric conductance

13. The value $6.6720 \times 10^{-11}$ $Nm^2kg^{-2}$ pertains to:
    (a) Faraday constant           (b) Boltzmann constant
    (c) molar gas constant         (d) gravitational constant

14. What do the symbols u, d, c, s, t, b, represent?
    (a) quarks                     (b) atomic sub-shells
    (c) vector notations
    (d) symbols used in equations of motion

15. In the adjoining n-p-n type semiconductor device what do the letters A, B, and C represent?
    (a) base, collector, emitter  (b) collector, base, emitter
    (c) emitter, collector, base
    (d) emitter, base, collector

16. A photodiode is symbolised by the figure:

(a) 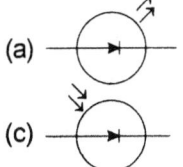          (b)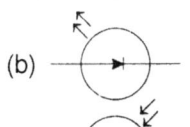

(c)                                (d)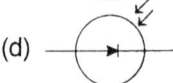

17. The symbol for the massive unstable elementary particle first detected in the year 1974 is:
    (a) J
    (b) 'Ψ'
    (c) either j or 'Ψ'
    (d) neither J nor 'Ψ'

18. To which category of particles do $\Sigma^+$, $\Sigma^0$, $\Sigma^{-1}$ belong?
    (a) leptons
    (b) baryons
    (c) mesons
    (d) photons

19. In the term 'myriametric' wave, what does the prefix 'myria' indicate?
    (a) 1 km
    (b) 10 km
    (c) 100 km
    (d) 1000 m

20. Which among the following Greek alphabets symbolises these physical quantities: pulsatance, solid angle, dispersive power, and angular velocity?
    (a) Δ
    (b) Ψ
    (c) λ
    (d) Ω

# 5

# CLASSICAL MECHANICS

1. A man holding two equal masses on his stretched arms is being rotated on a turn-table at some angular speed. Without bending his arms, he just lets the two masses fall. How does his angular speed change?
   (a) It decreases
   (b) It increases
   (c) It remains unaffected
   (d) It becomes zero

2. The equation, $y = bx - cx^2$, shows that the path traced by a moving body is:
   (a) a circle
   (b) an ellipse
   (c) a parabola
   (d) a hyperbola

3. Two bodies, 'A' and 'B', of masses '2m' and 'm' are released simultaneously from heights '$h_1$', and '$h_2$', respectively. What will be the ratio of time taken by the bodies 'A' and 'B' to reach the ground?
   (a) $\sqrt{h_1} : \sqrt{h_2}$          (b) $h_1 : h_2$
   (c) $h_1 : 2h_2$          (d) $2h_1 : h_2$

4. A body floats in a liquid kept in a beaker. The whole system falls freely under the action of gravity. The upthrust on the body due to the liquid is:
   (a) equal to the weight of liquid displaced.
   (b) equal to the weight of immersed portion of the body.
   (c) equal to the weight of the body in air.
   (d) zero.

5. From Newton's laws of motion, one can infer that:
   I.   Newton's first law describes the motion of a body free of external forces.
   II.  Newton's second law relates force to motion.
   III. Newton's third law is not directly a statement about motion, but a statement about forces in motion.
   IV.  Newton's third law leads to the principle of conservation of momentum.

   Which combination of the above statements is true?
   (a) I, II and III only        (b) I, II and IV only
   (c) II, III and IV only       (d) I, II, III and IV

6. Some mercury droplets coalesce to form a single big drop. The temperature of the big drop will:
   (a) increase
   (b) decrease
   (c) first decrease and then increase
   (d) remain the same

7. If impulse is:
   (a) positive, the momentum of the body decreases.
   (b) negative, the momentum of the body increases.
   (c) infinity, the momentum of the body becomes infinite.
   (d) zero, the momentum of the body becomes zero.

8. A man standing on a small weighing machine inside a moving lift notices that his weight is increasing. What do you conclude?
   (a) The lift is going down with an acceleration.
   (b) The lift is going up with an acceleration.
   (c) The lift is going down with uniform speed.
   (d) The lift is going up with uniform speed.

9. Two bodies of masses M and 2M are moving in opposite direction with velocities 2V and V respectively. On collision, they stick together to form one body. What will be the velocity of this compact mass after the collision?
   (a) V
   (b) 2V
   (c) 3V
   (d) 0

10. In which of the following cases, the moment of inertia is greatest?
   I.  A thin circular ring of radius R and mass M rotating about its diameter.
   II. A circular disc of radius R and mass M rotating about a direction perpendicular to disc at its centre.
   III. A solid cylinder of radius R and mass M rotating about the axis of cylinder.

   (a) I
   (b) II
   (c) III
   (d) Same in all the cases

11. What will be the ratio of the radii of two spheres—one solid and the other hollow—having the same mass, same kinetic energy or rotation, and the same angular velocity about a common axis through their centres?
   (a) $\sqrt{3} : \sqrt{5}$
   (b) $\sqrt{5} : \sqrt{3}$
   (c) $5 : 3$
   (d) $3 : 5$

12. A solid ball of mass 5 kg moving with velocity V hits a stationary pingpong ball of mass 5 g. What will be the speed of the lighter ball after the collision?

(a) V/4                            (b) V/2

(c) V                                (d) 2V

13. An air-bubble rises from the bottom of a long and narrow glass tube full of glycerene. What happens to the speed of the air-bubble till it comes to the top?

(a) It first increases, then moves up with constant velocity.
(b) It goes on decreasing.
(c) It goes on increasing.
(d) The speed remains the same throughout.

14. The angular momentum of a body is a measure of the strength of its rotational tendency about a fixed point. Which of the following statements is wrong for a rotating wheel?

(a) Greater its mass the greater is the angular momentum.
(b) Greater its moment of inertia the smaller is the angular momentum.
(c) Greater the distance from the reference point, greater is the angular momentum.
(d) Greater the perpendicular component of its velocity, greater is the angular momentum.

15. The relative densities of three liquids X, Y and Z are 0.7, 1.2, and 1.7 respectively. A small rod floats vertically just fully immersed in the liquid Y. Which of the following set of diagrams illustrates the equilibrium positions of the rod in the liquids X and Z?

(a) 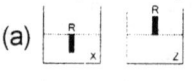           (b)

(c) 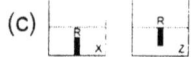           (d)

16. A particle 'P' is attached to a string and describes a circle of radius 'r' in a vertical plane. Which statement regarding the tension in the string is wrong?

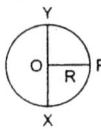

(a) At the highest point Y the tension acts along the radius in the downward direction.
(b) At the lowest point X the tension acts in the upward direction.
(c) Tension in the string is lowest at the highest point.
(d) Tension in the string is lowest at the highest point of the curve and is maximum at the lowest position on the curve.

17. The cooling curve below suggests that the melting point of naphthalene is:

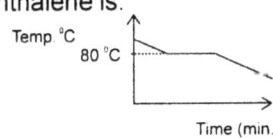

(a) 40 K                    (b) 80 K
(c) 353 K                   (d) 373 K

18. A person may feel weightlessness, if:
    I.   he is in a spaceship orbiting round the earth.
    II.  he manages to go to the centre of the earth.
    III. he falls freely from some height.
    IV.  a lift in which he is standing is coming down with an acceleration equal to the acceleration due to gravity.

    Which combination is correct?
    (a) I, II and III          (b) I, III and IV
    (c) II, III and IV         (d) I, II, III and IV

19. Force required to double the length of a wire of unit cross-section is numerically equal to.
    (a) bulk modulus
    (b) Young' modulus
    (c) modulus of rigidity
    (d) Poisson's ratio

20. The period of oscillation of a simple pendulum is doubled when:
    (a) the amplitude is doubled.
    (b) the length is doubled.
    (c) the length is made four times.
    (d) the mass of the bob of the pendulum is doubled.

# 6

## DOMAIN OF THE FORCES

1.  The four basic forces in nature are:
    I.   gravitational force    II.  electromagnetic force
    III. strong nuclear force    IV. weak nuclear force

    The relative magnitudes of these forces are in the order of
    (a) I > II > III > IV      (b) III > II > IV > I
    (c) III > II > I > IV      (d) III > I > II > IV

2.  Between different layers of fluid in relative motion, viscosity introduces:
    (a) intermolecular force      (b) radial force
    (c) cohesive force      (d) tangential force

3.  The production of electric charge on a conductor under the influence of an electric field is called:
    (a) electrostriction
    (b) electromagnetic induction
    (c) electrostatic induction
    (d) electromagnetic interaction

4.  The natural force that acts over a distance that is less than 0.000 000 000 000 001 metres is known as:
    (a) nuclear force      (b) coulombian force
    (c) gravitational force      (d) leptonic force

5. The gravitational force with which a body is attracted towards the earth is:
    (a) maximum at the equator and minimum at the poles.
    (b) minimum at the equator and maximum at the poles.
    (c) the same at all the places on the earth's surface.
    (d) independent of the place on the earth's surface.

6. Two parallel wires carrying currents in the same direction:
    (a) repel each other due to electric force between them.
    (b) repel each other due to magnetic force between them.
    (c) attract each other due to electric force between them.
    (d) attract each other due to magnetic force between them.

7. The force that holds nucleons together is called:
    (a) electrostatic force          (b) strong nuclear force
    (c) weak nuclear force          (d) internuclear force

8. Nuclear forces are:
    (a) strong and long-ranged
    (b) strong and short-ranged
    (c) weak and long-ranged
    (d) weak and short-ranged

9. A force between a body and the air caused by their relative motion is known as:
    (a) drag force                  (b) aerodynamic force
    (c) lift force                  (d) wind stress

10. The electrostatic force between two electrons is 'F'. What will be the electrostatic force between two protons at the same distance?
    (a) –F                          (b) F
    (c) –1836 F                     (d) 1836 F

11. A retarding force that acts upon a body moving through a gaseous medium in a direction opposite to the motion of the body is called:
    (a) friction drag          (b) pressure drag
    (c) aerodynamic drag       (d) wave drag

12. Read the following statements:
    I.   A magnetic field is unable to penetrate into a superconductor.
    II.  An electric field can be cut off by a screen of conducting material.
    III. Gravitational field can be freely transmitted through all bodies.

    Which statement is false?
    (a) I                      (b) II
    (c) III                    (d) None of these

13. A method of opposing the force of gravity using the mutual repulsion between two like magnetic poles is called:
    (a) magnetic escapement    (b) magnetic suspension
    (c) magnetic levitation    (d) magnetic rotation

14. The interaction between electron and neutrino in radioactive decay is:
    (a) a leptonic force       (b) a hadronic force
    (c) an electrostatic force (d) an electromagnetic force

15. The migration of fine particles of a solid suspended in a liquid to the anode or cathode when an electric field is applied to the suspension is called:
    (a) cataphoresis           (b) electrophoresis
    (c) anaphoresis            (d) electroviscosity

16. Which of the following shows that there must be a force acting on the earth and directed towards the sun?
    (a) Revolution of the earth round the sun.
    (b) Apparent motion of the sun round the earth.
    (c) Phenomena of day and night.
    (d) Rotation of earth about its axis.

17. Name the theory which attempts to link all the four fundamental forces of nature:
    (a) centrosymmetry
    (b) unitary symmetry
    (c) space reflection symmetry
    (d) supersymmetry

18. 'Hypercharge', the hypothetical fifth force of nature, was discovered by Ephraim Fishbach in 1986. What is its nature?
    (a) It enhances gravity.
    (b) It acts perpendicular to gravity.
    (c) It acts counter to gravity.
    (d) It nullifies gravity.

19. An exchange force between nucleons in which charge is exchanged is called:
    (a) Majorana force     (b) Heisenberg force
    (c) Wiegner force      (d) Bartlett force

20. Which of the following among Newton's laws gives the definition of 'force'?
    (a) First law of motion     (b) Second law of motion
    (c) Third law of motion     (d) None of the above

# 7

## ENERGY SCENARIO

1. 'Total energy of an ideal liquid under streamline flow remains constant.' This is known as:
   - (a) Torricelli's theorem
   - (b) Bernoulli's theorem
   - (c) Poiseuille's theorem
   - (d) Carnot's theorem

2. The energy required to remove an electron from an atom is called:
   - (a) excitation energy
   - (b) mechanical energy
   - (c) threshold energy
   - (d) ionisation energy

3. The energy consumed in magnetising and demagnetising magnetic material is called:
   - (a) core loss
   - (b) copper loss
   - (c) hysteresis loss
   - (d) eddy current loss

4. What do you call an electronic circuit that converts energy from a direct current source into a periodically varying electrical output?
   - (a) oscillator
   - (b) oscillograph
   - (c) oscilloscope
   - (d) oscillogram

5. Who was the first physicist to theorise that light energy is a stream of rapid electric and magnetic oscillations?
   - (a) Heinrich Hertz
   - (b) Arthur Crompton
   - (c) Enrico Fermi
   - (d) James Clerk Maxwell

6. Energy of a photon is expressed by:
   (a) $E = 1/2\, m\, v^2$               (b) $E = mc^2$
   (c) $E = h\upsilon^2$                (d) $E = mgh$

7. Energy of an electron is taken as zero when it is:
   (a) in its ground state      (b) far away from the nucleus
   (c) in the K-shell            (d) in the orbit

8. What is the total energy of an electron around the nucleus?
   (a) Zero                 (b) Less than zero
   (c) More than zero        (d) Always varying

9. An energy equivalent of about $10^{22}$ J pertains to:
   (a) daily energy output of the sun
   (b) kinetic energy of the earth's rotation about the sun
   (c) energy equivalent of the sun's mass
   (d) solar energy received per day on the earth

10. In a solid, an unfilled vacancy in an electronic energy level is called:
    (a) minority carrier       (b) majority carrier
    (c) hole                  (d) electron

11. When an electron falls back from an excited state to the ground state, light is produced. In the following diagram, which visible light is produced?

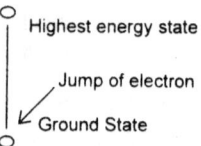

    (a) blue light           (b) green light
    (c) yellow light         (d) red light

12. The whole mass of an electron is converted into energy by:
    (a) increasing its velocity so that it moves with the velocity of light.
    (b) accelerating it by a high potential in a betatron.
    (c) combining it with a positron.
    (d) interacting it with beta rays.

13. The type of light that is made of only one wavelength and all the photons leave their source in a synchronised manner, travelling in a narrow beam, is called:
    (a) polarised electromagnetic radiation
    (b) laser
    (c) maser
    (d) Cherenkov radiation

14. Normally, electrons remain in an excited state for a short period. They can be made to remain in a unique excited state for a very long duration. This is known as:
    (a) stimulated emission
    (b) stimulated absorption
    (c) optical pumping
    (d) population inversion

15. The exchange of energy between one particle and an electromagnetic wave is called:
    (a) radiation heat          (b) interference
    (c) internal energy         (d) internal conversion

16. The amount of potential energy stored in an elastic substance by means of elastic deformation is called:
    (a) decalescence            (b) bulk energy
    (c) resilience              (d) internal energy

17. The rate at which energy is radiated by a body depends upon:
    (a) the nature of the surface
    (b) the area of the surface
    (c) the temperature of the surface
    (d) all the above factors

18. The gravitational potential energy of the known universe is in the range:
    (a) $10^{68}$ J
    (b) $10^{78}$ J
    (c) $10^{88}$ J
    (d) $10^{98}$ J

19. What happens to the kinetic energy of a bullet when it rises vertically upward?
    (a) It increases
    (b) It decreases
    (c) It remains the same
    (d) It becomes zero

20. What is the shape of the graph between the speed and kinetic energy of a body?
    (a) a straight line
    (b) parabola
    (c) hyperbola
    (d) none of the above

# 8

# CAUSE AND EFFECT

1. If a current-carrying conductor is placed in a magnetic field and oriented so that the field is at right angles to the direction of the current, an electric field is produced in the conductor perpendicular to both the current and the magnetic field. This is summarised in:
   (a) Magnus effect      (b) Hall effect
   (c) Ferranti effect
   (d) Corbino effect

2. Third law of thermodynamics is also known as:
   (a) Principle of conservation of energy
   (b) Claussius' virial law
   (c) Nernst heat theorem
   (d) Boltzmann principle

3. When heat flows through a metallic strip in a magnetic field, the direction of flow being across the lines of force, an emf is developed perpendicular to both the flow and the lines of force. This effect is called:
   (a) Nernst effect
   (b) Leduce effect
   (c) Righi effect
   (d) Gibbs–Helmholtz effect

4. A long iron cylinder rotating at high speed about its longitudinal axis develops a slight magnetisation which increases with the angular speed of rotation. This effect is known as:
   (a) Barnett effect
   (b) Barkhausen effect
   (c) Ettinghausen effect
   (d) Einstein and de Haas effect

5. The entropy of a substance approaches zero as its temperature approaches absolute zero. This is:
   (a) zeroeth law of thermodynamics
   (b) first law of thermodynamics
   (c) second law of thermodynamics
   (d) third law of thermodynamics

6. From Wien's displacement law, it is concluded that an extremely hot star appears to be:
   (a) red                     (b) white
   (c) violet                  (d) orange

7. The splitting of the spectral lines in the presence of magnetic field is called:
   (a) Zeeman effect           (b) Stark effect
   (c) Compton effect
   (d) Paschen–Back effect

8. The square root of the frequency of the characteristic lines in the X-ray spectrum is directly proportional to the atomic number of the element. This law is known as:
   (a) Bragg's law             (b) Compton's law
   (c) Moseley's law           (d) Knipping–Laue law

9. A magnetostatic effect concerned with the double refraction of light in a liquid when the liquid is placed in a transverse magnetic field is known as:
   (a) Cotton–Mouton effect   (b) Cotton effect
   (c) Kerr effect             (d) Faraday effect

10. The magnetic field due to current flowing in a long straight conductor is directly proportional to the distance of the point of observation from the conductor. What is this law known as?
   (a) Beer–Lambert law       (b) Biot–Savart's law
   (c) Blonde–Rey law         (d) Ampère's law

11. No engine can be more efficient than a reversible engine working between the same temperature. This is the essence of:
   (a) Carathéodory's principle
   (b) Clausius' law
   (c) Kopp and Neumann's law
   (d) Carnot's theorem

12. An increase in wavelength that occurs when radiation is scattered by free electrons. This is summed up in:
   (a) Mie scattering
   (b) Rayleigh scattering
   (c) Compton effect
   (d) Delbruck scattering

13. If a piezoelectric crystal is placed in a liquid and vibrated at a fixed frequency it sets up acoustic waves. This is known as:
   (a) Debye-Sears effect     (b) Kerr effect
   (c) Pockells effect        (d) Faraday effect

14. Total electric flux acting normally to any closed surface drawn in an electric field is equal to the total change of electricity inside the closed surface. This is known as:
    (a) Gauss' theorem           (b) Stokes' theorem
    (c) Poynting's theorem       (d) Green's theorem

15. The ratio of the thermal to electrical conductivity of all pure metals at a given temperature is approximately constant. This is summarised in:
    (a) Wertheims' law
    (b) Wiedemann–Franz law
    (c) Wien's law
    (d) Wigner effect

16. No two fermions can exist in identical quantum states. This is known as:
    (a) Fermi–Dirac distribution law
    (b) Fermi gas theory
    (c) Pauli exclusion principle
    (d) Fermi–Dirac–Sommerfeld law

17. What is the name of the hypothetical theory that would unify all the fundamental forces of nature?
    (a) Classical field theory
    (b) Unified field theory
    (c) Grand unified theory
    (d) Super grand unified theory

18. The Weinberg and Salam theory unifying electromagnetic forces and weak nuclear interactions is known as:
    (a) Electroweak theory       (b) Eight-fold theory
    (c) Supersymmetry            (d) Unitarity

19. When a superconducting material is cooled below its critical temperature in the presence of an applied magnetic field, it expels all magnetic flux from its interior. This is known as:
    (a) Ochsenfeld effect
    (b) Ginzburg–Landau effect
    (c) Meissner effect
    (d) Jodrphdon effect

20. A reduction of the work function of a solid due to the application of an external electric field leading to a consequent increase in its electron emission is called:
    (a) Schottky effect
    (b) Johnson–Rahbeck effect
    (c) Ferranti effect
    (d) Wilson effect

# 9

# IDEAS IN ACTION

1.  On which principle does an electron microscope work?
    (a) Wave-like properties of moving electrons
    (b) Dual nature of moving electrons
    (c) Particle nature of moving electrons
    (d) Microradiography

2.  Name the instrument for observing a moving body by making it visible intermittently and thereby giving it the optical illusion of being stationary:
    (a) hodoscope          (b) periscope
    (c) stroboscope        (d) gyroscope

3.  An electronic tube which produces high-frequency microwave oscillations is called:
    (a) magneton           (b) magneto
    (c) magnetron          (d) magnox

4.  What do we call a four-arm bridge used for measuring self-inductance?
    (a) Anderson bridge    (b) Owen bridge
    (c) Wheatstone bridge  (d) Carey Foster bridge

5. What name is given to the simple pendulum in which the bob swings in a horizontal circle?
   (a) conical pendulum
   (b) horizontal pendulum
   (c) compound pendulum
   (d) galitzin pendulum

6. Which device is used for converting a non-electrical parameter into electrical signals?
   (a) transductor
   (b) transducer
   (c) transistor
   (d) transformer

7. What is the name of the instrument for monitoring elastic properties of microscopic scale?
   (a) Phase-contrast microscope
   (b) Electron microscope
   (c) Acoustic microscope
   (d) Interference microsope

8. Which of the following is a multiple-beam interferometer?
   (a) Fabry–Perot interferometer
   (b) Mach–Zehnder interferometer
   (c) Twyman–Green interferometer
   (d) Michelson interferometer

9. Which of the following devices is employed for the measurement of the momentum of a bullet?
   (a) Foucault's pendulum
   (b) Ballistic pendulum
   (c) Schuler pendulum
   (d) Kater's reversible pendulum

10. Name the instrument which measures the angular speed of a rotating shaft:
    (a) tachometer
    (b) tacheometer
    (c) tachymeter
    (d) tachiloscope

11. A flexible device of connective links used to transmit power is called:
    (a) gear drive
    (b) belt drive
    (c) chain drive
    (d) block and tackle

12. What is a coronagraph?
    (a) An astronomical telescope used for observation of the solar corona.
    (b) A device for recording the epoch of an event.
    (c) A device to observe the coloured rings round the sun or the moon.
    (d) An instrument to record heat disorders.

13. A machine for accelerating charged particles to very high energies is known as:
    (a) cyclotron
    (b) synchrotron
    (c) synchrocyclotron
    (d) thyratron

14. Boy's camera is used for photographing:
    (a) minute objects
    (b) fast-moving objects
    (c) underwater objects
    (d) lightning flashes

15. Name the instrument for measuring the intensity of direct solar radiation at normal incidence:
    (a) solarimeter
    (b) pyrometer
    (c) pyranometer
    (d) pyreheliometer

16. The total reflection prism used in the prismatic telescopes and binoculars is called:
    (a) Nicol prism
    (b) Rochon prism
    (c) Porro prism
    (d) Wollaston prism

17. Ultrasonic frequencies may be generated by:
    I.   Galton whistle
    II.  Hartmann oscillator
    III. Piezoelectric oscillator

    Which combination is correct?
    (a) I and II only          (b) I and III only
    (c) II and III only        (d) I, II and III

18. What is auxometer?
    (a) An instrument for measuring the rate of flow of a gas.
    (b) An apparatus for measuring the magnifying power of an optical system.
    (c) A device for recording the elongation of a thin sheet by means of a lever and smoked drum.
    (d) An instrument to measure the contraction of muscles.

19. Name the machine that accelerates protons to energies greater than 3 GeV:
    (a) Cosmotron            (b) Isotron
    (c) Gyrotron             (d) Bevatron

20. The Arecibo Ionospheric Observatory is the site of the world's largest radio–radar telescope. The immovable dish of the telescope is cradled in a natural bowl. It has been used occasionally to search for signals from other extra-terrestrial intelligent beings. Where is this observatory situated?
    (a) Chile               (b) New Mexico
    (c) California          (d) Puerto Rico

# 10

# PHYSICAL PHENOMENA

1. Diffraction phenomenon associated with a point source of light which produces curved wavefronts is known as:
   (a) Fraunhofer diffraction   (b) electron diffraction
   (c) Fresnel diffraction       (d) neutron diffraction

2. Specific orientation of electric and magnetic fields of electromagnetic wave is known as:
   (a) interference
   (b) electromagnetic induction
   (c) polarisation
   (d) electromagnetic separation

3. The production of small flashes of light from certain materials as a result of the impact of radiation is called:
   (a) scintillation              (b) luminance
   (c) luminescence               (d) fluorescence

4. The scattering of the charged particles by nuclei due to electrostatic forces between them is called:
   (a) electrostatic deflection  (b) Coulomb scattering
   (c) elastic scattering         (d) Mie scattering

5. The leakage of gas through a fine orifice is called:
   (a) emission          (b) diffusion
   (c) effusion          (d) dissipation

6. A feeble light emitted from the anode of some cells is called:
   (a) electroradiescence
   (b) radioluminescence
   (c) eletrothermoluminescence
   (d) galvanoluminescence

7. The migration of fine particles of solid suspended in liquid to the anode or cathode when an electric field is applied to the suspension is known as:
   (a) electrophoresis     (b) cataphoresis
   (c) anaphoresis         (d) electrolysis

8. What is the phenomenon shown by ferromagnetic substances whereby the magnetic flux through the medium depends on the magnetising field as well as the previous state of the substance?
   (a) Inversion           (b) Hysteresis
   (c) Irradiation         (d) Magnetostriction

9. The process of impressing one wave upon another of high frequency is called:
   (a) amplification       (b) rectification
   (c) modulation          (d) oscillation

10. The luminescence resulting from the bombardment of a substance with an electron beam is called:
    (a) incandescence
    (b) fluorescence
    (c) photoluminescence   (d) cathodoluminescence

11. The simultaneous formation of an electron and an anti-electron from a photon is known as:
    (a) annihilation          (b) mass defect
    (c) pair production        (d) fusion

12. Space reflection symmetry is called:
    (a) parallelism            (b) congruity
    (c) unity                  (d) parity

13. The emission of electromagnetic radiation from a substance due to non-thermal process is known as:
    (a) radiance               (b) luminescence
    (c) incandescence          (d) fluorescence

14. The change in electric resistance which ferromagnetic substances undergo when magnetised is called:
    (a) photoemission          (b) thermionic emission
    (c) thermal emission       (d) electro emission

15. The removal of electrons from a solid as a result of the temperature is called:
    (a) photodetachment        (b) photodisintegration
    (c) photofission           (d) photoionisation

16. The formation of a layer of foreign substance on an impermeable surface is known as:
    (a) absorption             (b) adsorption
    (c) advection              (d) permeability

17. A phenomenon in which a vibrating system responds with maximum amplitude to an alternating driving force is called:
    (a) echo                   (b) resonance
    (c) acoustic prolongation  (d) forced vibrations

18. The state when magnetic induction (B) as well as the magnetic field strength (H) are equal to zero is termed as:
    (a) dielectric loss          (b) magnetisation
    (c) demagnetisation          (d) magnetostriction

19. Nodding up and down motion of a spinning body as it precesses about its axis is called:
    (a) bobbing                  (b) nutation
    (c) gyration
    (d) precessional displacement

20. Name the phenomenon associated when a paramagnetic substance that contains unpaired electrons is subjected to high magnetic fields and microwave radiation:
    (a) Nuclear paramagnetic resonance
    (b) Nuclear magnetic resonance
    (c) Electron magnetic resonance
    (d) Electron spin resonance

# 11

# KITH AND KIN OF PHYSICS

1. Name the science which is concerned with the role of sound in the behaviour of living things:
   (a) Bionics
   (b) Bio-acoustics
   (c) Physiological acoustics
   (d) Psychoacoustics

2. What is the science that treats sound generation and transmission by fluid flow called?
   (a) Hydraulics          (b) Hydrology
   (c) Acoustics           (d) Aeroacoustics

3. What is metrology?
   (a) The science of measuring.
   (b) The study of earth's atmosphere.
   (c) The study of people's influx to a metropolitan city.
   (d) The study of meteors.

4. The science of electric charges in motion, without reference to the acompanying magnetic field is:
   (a) Electrokinetics        (b) Electrokinematics
   (c) Electrodynamics        (d) Electromagnetics

5. What is the branch of Physics that deals with the motion of free electrons under the influence of electric and magnetic fields leading to focusing and formation of images?
   (a) Electronics            (b) Electron Optics
   (c) Electromagnetism       (d) Solid State Physics

6. What is the science of surveying and mapping the earth's surface called?
   (a) Cartography            (b) Topography
   (c) Selenodesy             (d) Geodesy

7. The study of radiation from celestial sources at wavelengths shorter than 0.01 nm is called:
   (a) Astrophysics           (b) X-ray Astronomy
   (c) Radio Astronomy        (d) Gamma-ray Astronomy

8. What is the study of free atmosphere called?
   (a) Avionics               (b) Aerodynamics
   (c) Aerology               (d) Aetiology

9. What is the science of atoms and atomic theory called?
   (a) Atomic Physics         (b) Atomistics
   (c) Nuclear Physics        (d) Nucleonics

10. Fluidics deals with:
    (a) the science relating to the flow of fluids.
    (b) the study of motion produced in fluids by applied forces.
    (c) the study of liquid flow in tubes.
    (d) the study of properties, distribution, and utilisation of fluids.

11. Name the science of friction, lubrication, and wear of surfaces in relative motion?
    (a) Tribology
    (b) Tectonics
    (c) Fluidics
    (d) Pneumatics

12. What is the branch of Physics that deals with electron movement?
    (a) Atomics
    (b) Thermionics
    (c) Electronics
    (d) Atomechanics

13. What is the study of control and communications in complex electron systems and in animals?
    (a) Robotics
    (b) Cybernetics
    (c) Cryogenics
    (d) Ergonomics

14. What is the study of the deformation and flow of matter called?
    (a) Viscocity
    (b) Fluidics
    (c) Tribology
    (d) Rheology

15. Name the branch of Physics which explains the macroscopic properties of a system on the basis of the microscopic constituents of the system:
    (a) Statistical Mechanics (b) Celestial Mechanics
    (c) Quantum Mechanics    (d) Solid State Physics

16. What is the study of the Physical and thermodynamic properties of the atmosphere called?
    (a) Radar Meteorology
    (b) Rarefied Gas Dynamics
    (c) Plasma Physics
    (d) Psychrometrics

17. What is the science of graphic visualisation and interpretation of sound vibrations associated with each heartbeat?
    (a) Sound Spectrography (b) Acoustic Cardiography
    (c) Electrocardiography  (d) Phonocardiography

18. What is the study of rotating bodies called?
    (a) Gyrodynamics
    (b) Rotary Mechanics
    (c) Rotocraft–Lagrangian Mechanics
    (d) Spin Dynamics

19. What is the study of functions, characteristics and phenomena observed in the living world and the application of this knowledge to the world of machines called?
    (a) Bionomics          (b) Bionics
    (c) Bionomy            (d) Biophysics

20. What is the science of the nature of heavenly bodies called?
    (a) Cosmogony         (b) Cosmology
    (c) Cosmography       (d) Astrophysics

# 12

## VIBRANT PHYSICS

1. What is not true for a body executing simple harmonic motion?
   (a) The acceleration is independent of time.
   (b) The oscillations are periodic.
   (c) The acceleration acts in a direction opposite to that of the displacement.
   (d) The restoring force is proportional to the displacement.

2. Of the following properties of a wave the one that is independent of the other is:
   (a) frequency          (b) wavelength
   (c) velocity           (d) amplitude

3. Name the electromagnetic radiation in which wavelengths lie in the range from about 1 micrometer to 1 millimetre:
   (a) radiowave          (b) microwave
   (c) infra-red          (d) ultraviolet

4. Electromagnetic radiations in the wavelength range 4–400 nm are called:
   (a) ultraviolet radiations    (b) infra-red radiations
   (c) visible radiations        (d) X-rays

5. Frequency of about $10^{10}$ Hz is known as:
   (a) infrasonic              (b) ultrasonic
   (c) supersonic              (d) pretersonic

6. Beta rays emitted by a radioactive material are:
   (a) electromagnetic radiations
   (b) neutral particles
   (c) charged particles emitted by the nucleus
   (d) electrons orbiting around the nucleus

7. The process of impressing one wave system on another
   of higher frequency is called:
   (a) inflexion               (b) modulation
   (c) transposition           (d) alteration

8. The scattering of light by particles of smaller dimensions
   compared with the wavelength of light is known as:
   (a) Rayleigh scattering
   (b) Mie scattering
   (c) Compton scattering
   (d) Raman scattering

9. The electromagnetic radiations emitted by electrons
   when they pass through matter are called:
   (a) Cerenkov radiations     (b) delta rays
   (c) Bremsstrahlung          (d) canal rays

10. Which solar radiation interacting with vapour clouds of
    methane, water, gases, etc., caused the production of
    amino acids which eventually originated life on our
    planet?
    (a) Cosmic radiations      (b) Gamma rays
    (c) Ultraviolet radiations (d) Infra-red radiations

11. Speed of sound wave may depend on the following:
    I.   It is independent of pressure of the gas at constant temperature.
    II.  It is directly proportional to the square-root of temperature in absolute scale.
    III. It is inversely proportional to the density of the gas through which it passes.
    IV.  It increases due to the pressure of water vapour.

    Which combination is correct?
    (a) I, II, and III            (b) I, II, and IV
    (c) II, III, and IV           (d) I, II, III, and IV

12. The displacement pattern traced out by the super-imposition of two vibrations in directions at right angles to each other is called:
    (a) Feynman diagrams          (b) Moire pattern
    (c) Lissajous's figures       (d) phase diagrams

13. The following figure depicts a wave travelling in a medium. Which pairs of particles are in phase?

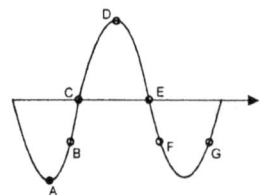

    (a) A and D                   (b) C and E
    (d) B and F                   (d) B and G

14. The natural frequency of vibration of a system is called:
    (a) period                    (b) eigenfunction
    (c) eigentone                 (d) resonance

15. The electromagnetic radiation originating electrical discharges in atmosphere is called:
    (a) microwaves        (b) sferics
    (c) atmospheric waves    (d) shockwaves

16. The electromagnetic radiation emitted by charged particles in circular motion at relativistic energies is called:
    (a) proton radiation
    (b) cycloradiation
    (c) synchrotron radiation
    (d) synchrocyclotron radiation

17. A nearly uniform flux of microwave radiation that is believed to permeate all of space is known as:
    (a) ether
    (b) cosmic background radiation
    (c) ylem
    (d) cosmic radiation

18. The following figure represents a wavefront AB which passes from air to another transparent medium and produces a new wavefront CD after refraction. The refractive index of the medium is:

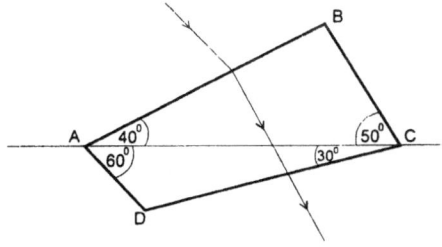

    (a) sin 40/ sin 30        (b) sin 50/ sin 30
    (c) sin 40/ sin 60        (d) sin 30/ sin 40

19. The equation x = a sin wt shows the variation of displacement of wave with time 't'. What does this equation represent?
    (a) Stationary wave
    (b) Progressive wave
    (c) Simple harmonic motion
    (d) Resonance-exponentially damped harmonic motion

20. Red, green and blue components of white light are incident on a filter $F_1$ which allows only red and blue colours. These two colours when strike another filter $F_2$ are completely absorbed by it. The filters $F_1$ and $F_2$ respectively are:

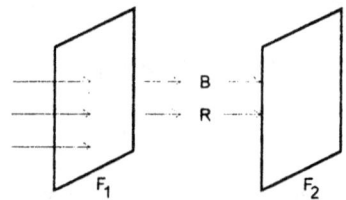

    (a) violet and green        (b) green and magenta
    (c) magenta and green       (d) orange and green

# 13

## MATERIAL PROPERTIES

1. A transparent material which has the property of storing electrical energy and releasing it as a visible light is called:
   (a) electrogen
   (b) electret
   (c) electrofluor
   (d) photocondenser

2. The response of a physical device to a unit change in the input is known as:
   (a) sensitivity
   (b) selectivity
   (c) reactivity
   (d) susceptibility

3. The condition of a body in which there are opposing physical properties at different points is known as:
   (a) antagonism
   (b) biformity
   (c) polarity
   (d) duplicity

4. The quality of variation of a physical property with the direction in a body along which the property is measured is called:
   (a) anisotropy
   (b) isotropy
   (c) directivity
   (d) orientation

5. The lagging of an effect behind the cause of the effect is known as:
   (a) consonance　　　　　　(b) remanence
   (c) superfluity　　　　　　(d) hysteresis

6. The property of a system that changes when the system undergoes a reversal change is called:
   (a) enthalpy　　　　　　　(b) epitaxy
   (c) entropy　　　　　　　(d) parity

7. The change in the physical or chemical properties of a solid substance due to radiation damage is represented by:
   (a) Wigner nuclides　　　　(b) Wigner energy
   (c) Wigner effect　　　　　(d) Wigner force

8. The property possessed by some substances to vary their flow of current under the influence of light is called:
   (a) photoemission　　　　(b) photoconductivity
   (c) photoelectricity
   (d) photoelectroluminescence

9. What is that property of solid in which stress and strain are not uniquely related in the pre-plastic range?
   (a) anelasticity　　　　　(b) resilience
   (c) tensility　　　　　　　(d) softness

10. What is the property of a substance which describes the magnetisation developed in that substance when excited by a source of a magnetomotive force?
    (a) susceptibility　　　　(b) porosity
    (c) permeability　　　　　(d) perforation

11. The property of material that has a negative magnetic susceptibiity so that the relative permeability is less than that of volume is known as:
    (a) diamagnetism          (b) ferrimagnetism
    (c) ferromagnetism
    (d) paramagnetism

12. What is not true about paramagnetic substances?
    (a) Paramagnetism is temperature dependent.
    (b) The magnetic susceptibility of paramagnetic substances has a small negative value.
    (c) When freely suspended in a uniform magnetic field, they align themselves parallel to the magnetic field.
    (d) They are feebly attracted by a magnet.

13. A property possessed by a current-carrying coil used as a measure of the magnetic strength is know as:
    (a) magnetic moment
    (b) magnetic dipole moment
    (c) electromagnetic moment
    (d) orbital magnetic moment

14. A relationship that exists between the right and a left hand of a body is called:
    (a) parity               (b) antiomorphy
    (c) enantiomorphy        (d) entropy

15. An objective description of the colour quality of a coloured light is called:
    (a) chromatism           (b) chromaticity
    (c) chrominance          (d) chroma

16. The property of a material by which it exhibits different colours in different chrystallographic direction on account of selective absorption of transmitted light is known as:
    (a) dichroism            (b) pleochroism
    (c) chrominance          (d) chromophobic

17. The property of quarks that allows them to be arranged in ways that seem to violate the exclusion principle is:
    (a) charm                (b) strangeness
    (c) truth                (d) beauty

18. Enhanced conductivity of semiconductors due to exposure to electromagnetic radiation is called:
    (a) photoconductivity    (b) radioconductivity
    (c) semiconductivity     (d) superconductivity

19. The electricity resulting from the application of mechanical pressure on a dielectric crystal is known as:
    (a) thermoelectricity    (b) static electricity
    (c) baroelectricity      (d) piezoelectricity

20. A property possessed by substances in which the atomic magnetic moments at low temperatures are arranged in a spiral is called:
    (a) helix magnetisation  (b) spiral magnetisation
    (c) helimagnetisation    (d) any of the above

# 14

## MICROCOSMOS

1. The charge on a particle is equal to $1.6 \times 10^{-19}$ C and is positive. What is this particle called?
   (a) electron
   (b) proton
   (c) positron
   (d) neutrino

2. Name the elementary particle having the following characteristics—charge: zero; spin: 1/2; stable when bound in nucleus; unstable when free:
   (a) Pi-zero meson
   (b) Xi-particle
   (c) neutrino
   (d) Psi-meson

3. Which of the following particles have zero rest mass?
   (a) neutrino and positron
   (b) photon and positron
   (c) neutron and neutrino
   (d) photon and neutrino

4. Neutrino is a particle having:
   (a) no charge but mass equal to electron.
   (b) no charge and no mass, but travels with the velocity of light.
   (c) no charge but having mass, and travels with the velocity of light.
   (d) no mass but charge equal to an electron.

5. When an alpha particle is emitted from a radioactive source:
   (a) its atomic number inceases by 2.
   (b) its atomic number decreases by 2.
   (c) its atomic number increases by 4.
   (d) its atomic number decreases by 4.

6. Two electrons present in the same orbital differ in their:
   (a) spin quantum number
   (b) magnetic quantum number
   (c) principal quantum number
   (d) azimuthal quantum number

7. Nuclear force is communicated from one nucleon to another via a particle called:
   (a) kaon                    (b) muon
   (c) pion                    (d) quark

8. A basic particle of which 'elementary particles' are believed to be composed of is termed as:
   (a) ylem                    (b) quark
   (c) gluon                   (d) graviton

9. The generic name for any hadronic particle with baryon number zero is:
   (a) meson                   (b) lepton
   (c) hadron                  (d) tauon

10. The only known elementary particle that has weak interactions is:
    (a) neutron                (b) neutrino
    (c) Omega minus            (d) Phi meson

11. The hypothetical core of a nucleus thought to be surrounded by a cloud of pions is called:
    (a) triton
    (b) nuclide
    (c) nuclei
    (d) nucleor

12. What is not common to pion and kaon?
    (a) Both are mesons
    (b) Both have zero spin
    (c) Both have antiparticles
    (d) Both are stable particles

13. An elementary particle that can take part in strong interaction is called:
    (a) lepton
    (b) hadron
    (c) hyperon
    (d) baryon

14. What are these: up, down, sideways, charm, top, bottom?
    (a) gluons
    (b) gravitons
    (c) ylem
    (d) quarks

15. What is not common to the following elementary particles: electron, neutrino, and muons? All these:
    (a) are stable particles.
    (b) are classified under leptons.
    (c) possess 1/2 spin.
    (d) except neutrino, have charge and mass.

16. What is not true about the following particles: muon, pion, and kaon?
    (a) Muon is a lepton while pion and kaon are mesons.
    (b) All are mesons.
    (c) Rest mass of muon is less than that of pion or kaon.
    (d) All of them have corresponding anti-particles.

17. A collective name for nucleons and other elementary particles that decay into nucleons by the emission of mesons is:
    (a) fermion　　　　　　　(b) boson
    (c) baryon　　　　　　　 (d) hadron

18. The hypothetical particle exchanged between quarks, building them together, is called:
    (a) gummon　　　　　　　(b) gluon
    (c) cementon　　　　　　 (d) paston

19. A hypothetical particle of time, equal to $10^{-24}$ second, i.e. the time taken for a photon to travel across an electron, is termed as:
    (a) epocon　　　　　　　 (b) ageon
    (c) hyperon　　　　　　　(d) chronon

20. The particles of gamma radiations are:
    (a) electrons　　　　　　(b) protons
    (c) neutrons　　　　　　 (d) photons

# 15

# MACROCOSMOS

1. A star containing about 1.5 solar masses (1 solar mass
   = 2 x $10^{30}$ kg) of material compressed into a volume of
   radius 10 km is known as:
   (a) white dwarf          (b) red giant
   (c) black hole           (d) neutron star

2. The first asteroid discovered was:
   (a) Hebe                 (b) Ceres
   (c) Pallas               (d) Eros

3. 'Alpha' ($\alpha$) in the nomenclature of the star system
   indicates:
   (a) biggest star         (b) smallest star
   (c) visibly brightest star   (d) visibly faintest star

4. Name the radio-astronomer who produced the first radio
   map of the universe:
   (a) Karl Jansky          (b) Ejnar Hertzsprung
   (c) Grote Reber          (d) Harlow Shapley

5. Which of the following is an example of a neutron star?
   (a) quasar               (b) pulsar
   (c) burster              (d) B.L. Lacertae object

6. The point at which a satellite launched from earth into lunar orbit is nearest to the surface of the moon is called:
   (a) aphelion
   (b) perihelion
   (c) pericynthion
   (d) apocynthion

7. The region in space around the sun, extending up to the planet Saturn and beyond, in which the effects of solar wind are strongly felt, is termed as:
   (a) heliosphere
   (b) photosphere
   (c) celestial sphere
   (d) chromosphere

8. What is NGC 224 or M 31?
   (a) Small Magellanic Cloud
   (b) Large Magellanic Cloud
   (c) Milky Way
   (d) Andromeda galaxy

9. Following factors may be responsible for the colour of a star:
   I.   The size of the star.
   II.  The distance of the star from the earth.
   III. The surface temperature of the star.

   Which combination is correct?
   (a) I only
   (b) II only
   (c) III only
   (d) I, II, and III

10. A small but heavy, invisible stellar object having such a strong pull of gravity that even light rays falling on it cannot escape is called:
    (a) black body
    (b) black hole
    (c) coronal hole
    (d) dark cloud

11. Pulsars are:
    I. sources of radiowaves.
    II. rapidly rotating neutron stars with intense magnetic field.
    III. so compressed that electrons and protons are forced to combine to form neutrons.

    Which combination is correct?
    (a) I only            (b) I and II only
    (c) I and III only    (d) I, II and III

12. The most distant discrete objects in the observable universe are:
    (a) quasars           (b) pulsars
    (c) radio galaxies    (d) B.L. Lacertae objects

13. Mapping of life of stars is drawn on:
    (a) Hertzsprung–Russel diagram
    (b) Hubble diagram
    (c) chromaticity diagram    (d) binding energy curve

14. Most of the stars when placed on the H–R diagrams fall in on a diagonal band known as:
    (a) the spectral class    (b) the Hertzsprung gap
    (c) the main sequence     (d) the forbidden band

15. Who was the first scientist to propose the idea of the Big Bang?
    (a) Abbe Lamaitre     (b) Thomas Gold
    (c) Hermann Bondi     (d) Alan Sandage

16. The Big Bang took place some 20 billion years ago. How long after that did the first stars begin to form?
    (a) 1 million years   (b) 5 million years
    (c) 1 billion years   (d) 4 billion years

17. Which of the following pairs is the strongest observational support in favour of the Big Bang theory of the universe?
    (a) Hubble's law, and presence of black holes.
    (b) Hubble's law, and cosmic background radiations.
    (c) Cosmic background radiations, and presence of black holes.
    (d) Hubble's law, and existence of pulsars.

18. In 1975, it was discovered through X-ray detecting satellite that the periodic bursts of X-rays are coming from a globular star cluster NGC 6624. What are these objects called?
    (a) pulsars              (b) quasars
    (c) bursters             (d) B.L. Lacertae objects

19. Who was the first astronomer to discover the 1987 A supernova in the Large Magellanic Cloud?
    (a) Albert Jones         (b) Ian Shelton
    (c) Guiseppe Piazzi      (d) David Gill

20. According to Walter Baade's nomenclature of stars, what is meant by 'member of Population I and Population II'?
    (a) The slow-moving stars are classified as members of Population I, and fast-moving stars are members of Population II.
    (b) The fast-moving stars belong to Population I and slow-moving stars belong to Population II.
    (c) Population I stars are found in the central regions of galaxies and in globular clusters where dust and gases are absent.
    (d) Population II stars include hot blue stars which are found in the arms of the spiral galaxies.

# 16

## LOGICAL PHYSICS

1  Supposing the earth suddenly contracts to half of its radius, what will be the length of the day?
   (a) 6 hours              (b) 8 hours
   (c) 12 hours             (d) no change

2. Four identical quadruplets, having same dimensions and same weights, are to jump on simultaneously to four different turn-tables that are originally rotating with same angular speed. The moment each of them lands on the turn-tables 'A' will stretch his arm, so will 'B' with two masses on each palm; 'C' will squeeze his arms, as also 'D' but with two masses on his palms.

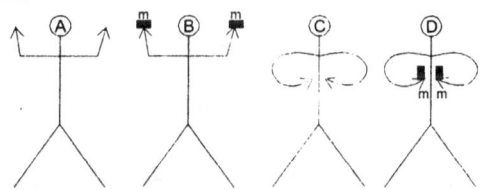

After a while, which of the quadruplets will rotate with greatest speed?
   (a) A                    (b) B
   (c) C                    (d) D

3. Electric currents with certain values are flowing in various branches of the following circuit:

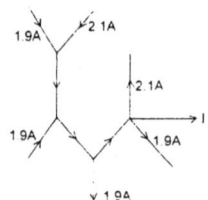

The value of current 'I' in the circuit is:
(a) zero                          (b) 0.2 Ampère
(c) 1.9 Ampère                    (d) 2.1 Ampère

4. Two positively charged spheres, attached to the same support through strings of the same lengths are taken to outer space in a spacecraft.

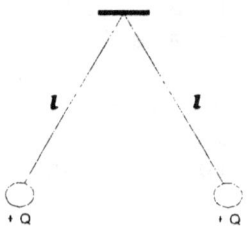

What will be the angle between the two strings?
(a) 0°                            (b) 60°
(c) 90°                           (d) 180°

5. Suppose (God forbid!) due to some reason, the earth expands to make its volume eight-fold. What do you expect your weight to be?
(a) one-fourth                    (b) one-half
(c) two-fold                      (d) unaffected

6.  In each of the following five pairs of balls, numbers 1 to 5, the balls undergo either electrostatic attraction ($\rightarrow\leftarrow$) or electrostatic repulsion ($\leftarrow\rightarrow$).

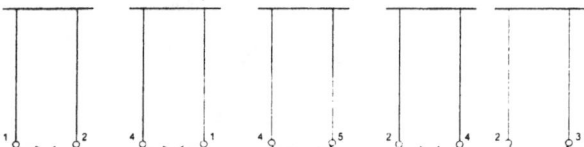

The ball numbered 1 must be:
(a) positively charged  (b) negatively charged
(c) either positively charged or negatively charged
(d) neutral

7.  The frequency of a pipe open at both the ends is 'f'. It is gradually dipped vertically in a water tub, till it is half-way through. What will be the new frequency of the vibrating column?

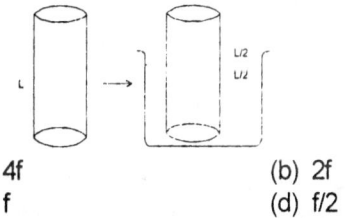

(a) 4f                          (b) 2f
(c) f                           (d) f/2

8.  A cube, a thin circular plate, and a sphere made of the same metal, have the same mass and same volume. They are initially heated to the same temperature. When left at room temperature, which of these bodies will cool fastest and slowest respectively?
(a) The circular plate; the sphere
(b) The circular plate; the cube
(c) The cube; the sphere
(d) The sphere; the circular plate

9. ABC is a right-angled prism. A ray PQ falling normally on one of its faces is found to suffer total internal reflection and emerges as QR.

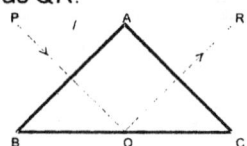

What is the minimum value of the refractive index of the material of the prism?

(a) $\sqrt{3} / 2$           (b) $\sqrt{2}$

(c) $1 / 2$             (d) $1 / \sqrt{2}$

10. Heat is developed in a metallic wire when some current flows through it. Following changes are made in the dimensions of the wire and the time for which the current passes:

I.   Its length and radius are reduced to half, and time of heat-flow also curtailed to half.

II.  Its length, radius, and the time for which heat flows are doubled.

III. Its length reduced to half, but the time of heat-flow is doubled.

Which of the following combinations justifies that the amount of heat produced remains the same as before?

(a) I and II only          (b) III only

(c) all the above         (d) none of the above

11. A shining metallic ball with a small black spot on its surface is heated to a very high temperature and then quickly taken to a dark room. Then:

(a) the spot appears darker than the ball.

(b) the spot appears brighter than the ball.

(c) both appear equally bright.

(d) both are invisible in the dark room.

12. Three steel wires have their lengths and diameters in the ratios 1:2:8 and 1:4:8 respectively, and are subjected to the same tension.

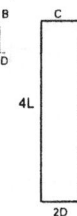

What will be the ratio of their elongation?
(a) 1:1:1             (b) 1:2:8
(c) 1:4:8             (d) 1:2:4

13. The focal length of an astronomical telescope is eleven times the focal length of the eye-piece. By some appropriate combinations of lenses, the focal length of the eye-piece is increased three times the previous value and the focal length of the objective is decreased in such a way that now the magnification is 3. What is the new length of the tube of telescope?
(a) It reduces to one-third of the previous length.
(b) It is doubled.
(c) It becomes three-fold.    (d) It remains the same.

14. A magnet is 'dipped' into a coil of wire, as shown in the following diagram:

The magnet falls with an acceleration:
(a) less than acceleration due to gravity 'g'
(b) greater than 'g'
(c) equal to 'g'             (d) zero

15. Sitar maestro Pandit Ravi Shankar is playing sitar, and you, as a physicist (unfortunately without musical ears!), observed the following oddities:
    I.   The greater the length of a vibrating string, the smaller its frequency.
    II.  The greater the tension in the string, the greater is the frequency.
    III. The heavier the mass of the string, the smaller the frequency.
    IV.  The thinner the wire, the higher its frequency.

    The maestro signalled which of the following combinations as the correct one:
    (a) I, II and III          (b) I, II and IV
    (c) II, III and IV         (d) I, II, III and IV

16. Four steel wires have their lengths in the ratios 1:2:3:4; their tensions in the ratios 16:9:4:1; and their radii in the ratios 4:3:2:1. What will be the ratios of their frequencies?
    (a) 1:1/2:1/3:1/4       (b) 1/2:1/3:1/4:1
    (c) 1/3:1/4:1:1/2       (d) 1/4:1:1/2:1/3

17. A motor cycle and a scooter are rotating about two adjacent round-abouts, with the same speed. The mass of the motor cycle is four times the mass of the scooter, but it is circling with half the velocity of the scooter. Which round-about has bigger diameter?
    (a) The one around which the scooterist is circling.
    (b) The one around which the motor cyclist is circling.
    (c) The round-abouts are of equal diameters.
    (d) The problem cannot be solved unless the inclinations to the verticle of the vehicles are not given.

18. You are cycling around a round-about with such constraints that the radius of the round-about, the velocity and the acceleration due to gravity have the same numeric value. If you calculate your inclination to the vertical, it would be:

(a) $0^0$                              (b) $45^0$

(c) $60^0$                             (d) $90^0$

19. What does the following nuclear reaction suggest?
$$_{17}Cl^{37} + {_1}H^2 = {_{18}}Ar^{38} + {_0}n^1$$

(a) Nuclear fission

(b) Nuclear fusion

(c) Transmutation of chlorine

(d) Synthesis of argon

20. Three strings 'A', 'B' and 'C' of same length are stretched on a sonometer. Their relative masses per unit length are 2:8:18 and their tensions are in the ratio 12:12:27. What is the ratio of the frequencies of note emitted by 'A', 'B' and 'C'?

(a) 1:1:1                           (b) 1:1:2

(c) 1.2:1                           (d) 2:1:1

# 17

# MAKERS OF PHYSICS

1. Besides working on high frequency alternating current, he invented the moving coil galvanometer. Who was he?
   (a) Jacques d'Arsonval
   (b) Luigi Aloisio Galvani
   (c) Hermann Ludwig Ferdinand Helmholtz
   (d) Willem Einthoven

2. Name the physicist who obtained the first coloured photographs of the solar system:
   (a) Ludwig Boltzmann      (b) Joseph Stefan
   (c) Gabriel Lippmann      (d) Auguste Marie Lumiere

3. Name the French physicist who helped Fresnel and Young to establish the wave theory of light, besides suggesting the rotating mirror method for determining the velocity of light:
   (a) Dominique Arago       (b) Jean Bernard Foucault
   (c) Armand Fizeau         (d) Olaus Roemer

4. Which British physicist investigated the ionised layers of the earth's atmosphere besides playing an important role in the development of RADAR?
   (a) Olever Heaviside      (b) Hans Friedrich Geitel
   (c) Edward Victor Appleton (d) Victor Hesse

5. He was the first to investigate the spectrum of the aurora borealis, and recognised the existence of hydrogen in the solar system. Who was this physicist whose name is associated with the spectroscopic unit of length?
   (a) Johann Balmer         (b) David Brewster
   (c) Joseph von Fraunhofer (d) Anders Jonas Ångström

6. He was a pioneer in the kinetic theory of gases. He contributed a lot to fluid mechanics and the theory of vibrating strings. Who was this founder of mathematical physics?
   (a) James Clerk Maxwell   (b) Daniel Bernoulli
   (c) Sir Isaac Newton      (d) Count Rumford

7. Who invented a torsion balance bearing his name, besides investigating gravitation and terrestrial magnetism?
   (a) Charles Vernon Boys
   (b) Henry Cavendish
   (c) Roland Baron von Evötvös
   (d) Hans Christian Oersted

8. Who introduced the idea of reversible cycles, besides developing the theory of heat engines?
   (a) Rudolf Clausius       (b) B.P.E. Clapeyron
   (c) Walter Nernst         (d) Sadi Nicolas Carnot

9. He was a professor of mathematics at St Petersburg University, professor of Anatomy and Physics at the University of Gröningen, and professor of Physics, Anatomy and Botany at the University of Basle. But he is most famous for what is known as 'Bernoulli's theorem'. Name this outstanding mathematician belonging to a well-known Swiss family:
   (a) Daniel Bernoulli      (b) Jacob Bernoulli
   (c) Johann Bernoulli      (d) none of the above

10. Who was the first to introduce the concept of 'dimensions' of a derived physical quantity in terms of fundamental quantities?
    (a) Jean Bapiste Joseph Fourier
    (b) Joseph Louis Lagrange
    (c) Pirce Simon, Marquis de Laplace
    (d) Gottfried Wilhelm Leibniz

11. Name the German physicist of the nineteenth century who was the key figure in the development of the famous optical firm of Carl Zeiss, Jena, besides designing a refractometer bearing his name, and improved many optical instruments?
    (a) Joseph Fraunhofer       (b) Ernst Abbe
    (c) G. Kirchhoff            (d) W.H. Wollaston

12. Who enunciated the principle of equipartition of energy?
    (a) Sir James Hopwood Jeans
    (b) Joseph Stefan
    (c) Ludwig Boltzmann
    (d) James Prescott Joule

13. He played a key part in establishing the wave theory of light and the conditions necessary for the two light beams to interference. A unit of frequency equal to $10^{12}$ Hz is named after him. Who was he?
    (a) Thomas Young            (b) Christiaan Huygens
    (c) Humphrey Lloyd          (d) Augustin Jean Fresnel

14. Apart from formulating his famous flux theorem bearing his name, he invented various types of magnetometers. He was also a famous astronomer of his time. Who was he?
    (a) E.E. Weber              (b) Karl Friedrich Gauss
    (c) James Clerk Maxwell     (d) Hans Christian Oersted

15. He is responsible for discovering over 5000 star clusters and nebulae, besides his discovery of the planet Uranus. He also showed for the first time that the solar spectrum contains infra-red rays. Who was this great astronomer?
    (a) Edmund Halley
    (b) Sir William Huggins
    (c) Sir James Hopwood Jeans
    (d) Sir William Herschel

16. An optician by profession, he did outstanding work in making telescopes and microscopes in the early nineteenth century, but his greatest achievement was to discover the dark lines in the solar system that bears his name. Who was he?
    (a) Anders Jonas Ångström
    (b) Ernest Abbe
    (c) Joseph von Fraunhofer  (d) William Hyde Wollaston

17. Besides formulating the theory of probabilites and contributing in the field of hydrostatics, he was the first to construct an ingenious calculating machine  Who was this philosopher–physicist who died when he was only 39 years old?
    (a) Charles Babbage       (b) Blaise Pascal
    (c) Pierre Fermat         (d) Gottfried Leibnitz

18. He introduced a triatomic theory of colour vision; he was the first to observe ocular astigmatism; he proved that the accommodation of eye was affected by change of curvature of the crystalline lens. But he is most famous for his discovery of interference of light and for developing the wave theory of light. Who was this physician-cum-physicist?
    (a) Christiaan Huygens    (b) Humphrey Lloyd
    (c) Augustin Jean Fresnel (d) Thomas Young

19 Crippled by Lou Gehrig's disease which made him handicapped to the extent that he cannot write, and can barely speak. This outstanding physicist is an authority on black hole. What is his name?

(a) Patrick Blackett      (b) Sheldon Glashow

(c) Stephen Hawking      (d) Leon Lederman

20. Name the brilliant physicist, who died at the young age of 32, but not before discovering a relation between frequency of characteristic X-rays emission and the atomic number of the element:

(a) Henry Gwyn–Jeffreys Moseley

(b) William Lawrence Bragg

(c) Arthur Crompton

(d) Max von Laue

## 18

# REASONING IN PHYSICS

1. An ice-skater rotates faster after drawing his hands inwards, because by doing so:
   - (a) his angular momentum increases.
   - (b) the air resistance decreases thereby his angular speed increases.
   - (c) he decreases his body volume thereby increasing his angular acceleration.
   - (d) he decreases his moment of inertia thereby increasing his angular velocity.

2. Why does a bicycle have spokes?
   - (a) Spokes increase the moment of inertia and so the bicycle runs smoother.
   - (b) Spokes add to the weight of the bicycle and so it has better equilibrium.
   - (c) Spokes help the wheels to run uniformly.
   - (d) Spokes keep the wheels in proper shape.

3. Which is more elastic—rubber or steel, and why?
   - (a) Rubber, because it has elastic property.
   - (b) Rubber, because for a given stress, it stretches more than steel.
   - (c) Steel, because it is denser than rubber.
   - (d) Steel, because for a given stress, the strain produced is less in steel than in rubber.

4. A ladder is more apt to slip when you are high on its rung than when you just begin to climb. Why?
   (a) As you climb up, your potential energy increases.
   (b) When you are high up, the ladder is in unstable equilibrium.
   (c) When you are high up, the moment of force tending to rotate the ladder about its base increases, while in the latter case, the moment of inertia is insufficient to cause slipping.
   (d) When you are high up, the centre of gravity of the system shifts upwards so the ladder is unstable, while in the latter case the system is more stable.

5. Electric power is transmitted over long distance through conducting wires of very high voltage, because:
   (a) of economical reasons.
   (b) signals of high voltages travel faster.
   (c) the power losses are reduced to minimum.
   (d) high voltages can be stepped down to desired levels easily.

6. Rain drops are spherical due to the tendency of liquid to have:
   (a) maximum density for a given volume.
   (b) minimum density for a given surface area.
   (c) minimum volume for a given surface area.
   (d) minimum surface area for a given volume.

7. Why does a green leaf look green in daylight?
   (a) It absorbs all the colours of white light except green which it reflects.
   (b) As compared to other colours, the green colour scatters more.
   (c) It has a biological reason, i.e. photosynthesis.
   (d) It reflects all the colours of white light except green, which it absorbs.

8. Why are the passengers in the upper deck of a double-decker bus not allowed to stand?
   (a) If the passengers are in standing position, they may start oscillating due to jerks and there is a possiblity of resonance, causing the bus to be toppled.
   (b) This ensures smaller centripetal force, thus helping the driver to negotiate the round-abouts properly.
   (c) This ensures that the centre of gravity of the system may not rise up and the bus may not be toppled due to unstable equilibrium.
   (d) This is just for safety.

9. Why is tungsten preferred as a filament in electric bulbs?
   (a) The resistance of tungsten is very high.
   (b) The melting point of tungsten is very high.
   (c) The electrical conductivity of tungsten is very high.
   (d) The tungsten filament can be fused with glass very easily.

10. Why are tuning forks made with definite frequencies in the order 256, 288, 320, 341, 384, 426, 480, and 512?
   (a) These frequencies are set according to the diatomic scale.
   (b) These numbers can be factorised easily.
   (c) These have been arbitrarily chosen as per international agreement.
   (d) These frequencies are within the audible range of human ears.

11. Electric current produces heat, then why is it that the lead wires carrying current are cold while the element of a heater is hot?
    (a) The element of a heater is thick so its resistance is small, hence more current flows through it than the lead wire.
    (b) The element of a heater is made of nichrome which has a low resistance as compared to the high resistance of lead wire; thus element draws more current.
    (c) The element of a heater is hot due to its high resistance, while the lead wire is cold due to its low resistance.
    (d) Due to low resistance the power generated in a heater's coil is more, but less in lead wire.

12. For linters, bridges, etc., why are the iron beams shaped? Because for a given length of beam. the depression will be small if:
    I.   iron has large Young's modulus.
    II.  the breadth of beam is small.
    III. the depth of beam is small.
    Which combination is correct?
    (a) I and II              (b) I and III
    (c) II and III            (d) I, II and III

13. Why does a ship made of steel float on water while an oil-pin of steel sink?
    (a) The ship contains large air pockets which help it to float smoothly.
    (b) Owing to the large volume of the ship, it displaces more water, so upthrust is more.
    (c) Density of sea water is greater and hence the ship floats.
    (d) In the case of a pin, the pressure is more since the area of its tip is small, so it sinks. But in the case of a ship the area of its base is more.

14. Inside the nucleus, protons are held together though they have the same charge. Why?
    (a) The electrostatic attractive force between an electron and a proton is more than the electrostatic repulsive force between the protons.
    (b) Neutrons prevent them from repelling each other.
    (c) The strong attractive nuclear force far exceeds the electrostatic force between the protons.
    (d) Gluons are responsible for holding them together.


15. In a telescope, why is the focal length of the objective lens large and that of the eye-piece small?
    (a) A telescope is meant to see distant objects, so objective lens has to be of greater focal length to gather more light.
    (b) This is essential to ensure a large magnification.
    (c) The distance between the objective lens and the eye-piece is the sum of their focal lengths, and since the eye-piece is of small focal length, the objective lens should be of greater focal length.
    (d) The statement is true only for astonomical telescopes.


16. Why are matter waves significant only in the motion of extremely small particles?
    (a) Small particles possess small kinetic energy.
    (b) Small particles are easily manageable.
    (c) Small particles have smaller mass and hence the de Broglie wavelength increases.
    (d) Extremely small particles possess small relativistic mass.

17. Why is phospher–brcnze alloy preferred as the suspension wire in suspension type of galvanometer? Following factors may be responsible for its preference:
    I.   It has a great tensile strength.
    II.  Its torsional couple per unit twist is small.
    III. It resists rust.
    IV.  Greater amount of phosphorus makes it shine.

    Which combination is correct?
    (a) I, II and III          (b) I, II and IV
    (c) I, III and IV          (d) II, III and IV

18. For inducing nuclear fission why is neutron considered as an ideal particle? Because:
    I.   it is a neutral particle.
    II.  it is not affected by the electric field of the positive nuclei.
    III. it can penetrate to a greater depth.
    IV.  it is a stable particle.

    Which combination is correct?
    (a) I, II and III          (b) I, II and IV
    (c) I, III and IV          (d) II, III and IV

19. Physics is sometimes referred to as exact science. Why?
    (a) Because it involves philosophy.
    (b) Due importance is given for the measurement of quantities.
    (c) Physics interacts with almost all the sciences.
    (d) Physics is related more closely to mathematics than any other science.

20. Change in frequency due to Doppler's effect is produced when:
    (a) the source and the observer are both at rest.
    (b) the source and the observer are moving in the same direction.
    (c) there is relative motion between the source and the observer.
    (d) there is resultant motion between the source and the observer.

# 19

# EXPERIMENTAL PHYSICS

1. While conducting experiment to find the specific charge (e/m), Sir J.J. Thomson observed that the ratio of the charge to mass of an electron is independent of:
   I.   the nature of gas.
   II.  the material of cathode.
   III. the voltage applied across the electrodes.

   Which of the following combinations is not correct?
   (a) I and II          (b) II and III
   (c) all the above     (d) none of the above

2. $1.76 \times 10^{11}$ Ckg$^{-1}$ is the ratio of charge of electron to its mass, which was experimentally found in 1896, using a discharge tube. Who conducted this classic experiment?
   (a) Johnston Stoney   (b) J.J. Thomson
   (c) R.A. Millikan     (d) C.T.R. Wilson

3. The first experiment to demonstrate the diffraction of electron is known as the:
   (a) Davisson–Germer experiment
   (b) Davis and Goucher's experiment
   (c) Bragg and Bragg experiment
   (d) Geiger–Marsden experiment

4. In an experiment to measure the velocity of electrons, an electric field (E) and a magnetic field (B) are employed to produce zero deflection. Then:
   (a) the two fields are parallel and the velocity is given by E/B.
   (b) the two fields are perpendicular and the velocity is given by E/B.
   (c) the two fields are parallel and the velocity is given by BE.
   (d) the two fields are perpendicular and the velocity is given by BE.

5. In an experiment, a uniform magnetic field is applied perpendicular to a horizontal beam of charged particles with constant velocity. Then the radius of curvature of the beam is directly proportional to its:
   (a) momentum          (b) energy
   (c) rest mass          (d) magnitude

6. In the Wilson cloud chamber experiment:
   (a) beta particles produce straighter tracks than alpha particles.
   (b) alpha particles produce straighter tracks than beta particles.
   (c) gamma particles produce straighter tracks than alpha particles.
   (d) alpha and beta particles do not produce straight tracks.

7. In Thomson's e/m experiment:
   (a) the electric and magnetic fields are perpendicular.
   (b) the electric and magnetic fields are parallel.
   (c) the uniform magnetic field is produced by a magnet.
   (d) the uniform magnetic field is produced by two parallel circular current-carrying coils.

8. The Geiger–Marsden experiment is concerned with the scattering of alpha particles. In which of the following metals is the deflection maximum?

(a) Gold             (b) Silver

(c) Copper         (d) Lead

9. The famous Michelson–Morley experiment was aimed at:

(a) detecting the hypothetical medium ether.

(b) measuring the motions of the earth through the ether.

(c) verifying Einstein's theory of relativity.

(d) determining the velocity of light.

10. X-rays were discovered by Wilhelm Roentgen, and were found to exhibit the properties of reflection, refraction, polarisation, interference and diffraction. Who was the first to determine the wavelengths of X-rays using a crystal and a three-dimensional diffraction grating?

(a) Maurice de Broglie

(b) Von Laue

(c) Karl Siegbahn

(d) Lawrence Bragg

11. An important experiment was conducted in 1914 to confirm Bohr's idea of energy levels by means of vapours under very low pressure. Which team of physicists conducted this experiment?

(a) Frank and Hertz

(b) Rydberg and Hertz

(c) Frank and Rydberg

(d) Frank, Hertz and Rydberg

12. Aston mass spectrograph is a device to measure the atomic masses of isotopes with great precision. Its principle consists in applying:
    (a) electric and magnetic fields simultaneously and in parallel direction.
    (b) electric and magnetic fields simultaneously in perpendicular direction.
    (c) successfully first the magnetic field and then the electric field at right angles to each other.
    (d) successfully first the electric field and then the magnetic field at right angles to each other.

13. Friedrich and Knipping experimentally confirmed that when X-rays fall on a single crystal, a series of symmetrically-arranged spots are recorded on a photosensitive film which help in recognising the type of the crystal and its structure. Who was the first to suggest this diffraction of X-rays with crystals?
    (a) Lawrence Bragg        (b) Max von Laue
    (c) Charles Barkla        (d) Henry Bragg

14. In order to confirm Einstein's theory of photo-electric effect, an experiment was conducted in 1916 using the alkali metals. Who conducted this experiment?
    (a) R.A. Millikan         (b) Philip Lenard
    (c) A.H. Compton          (d) W.H. Bragg

15. Cloud chamber technique is experimentally used for:
    (a) measurement of electronic mass.
    (b) measurement of electronic charge.
    (c) measurement of specific charge.
    (d) studying the interaction of charges in clouds.

16. The following figure is the outcome of the experimental investigation of the spectral distribution of energy in black body radiation. Which of the following scientists is not associated with the investigation?

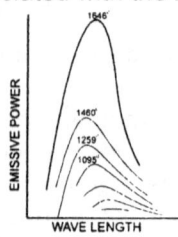

    (a) Rubens             (b) Karlbaum
    (c) Stefan             (d) Pringshelm

17. Experimental verification of quark was first carried out at:
    (a) CERN
    (b) SLAC
    (c) Fermi lab
    (d) Petra accelerator in Hamburg

18. Experiments UA 1 (underground area 1) and UA 2 (underground area 2), led respectively by Carlo Rubbia and Pierre Darriulat in early 1980s were conducted to discover:
    (a) top quark            (b) Z boson
    (c) W and Z particles    (d) Xi particle

19. Which of the following is the largest experimental project for observing the proton decay?
    (a) I.M.B. detector under Lake Erie, Ohio
    (b) Kamioka detector, Japan
    (c) Kolar Gold Mine, India
    (d) Homestake Gold Mine, South Dakota

20. A historical experiment was announced on 6 November 1919 by two British teams, who observed that light coming from stars bends as it passes near the sun during a total eclipse. What hypothesis this experiment proved?
    (a) There is no such thing as ether.
    (b) Light is electromagnetic in nature.
    (c) Space is curved.
    (d) The velocity of light is maximum.

# 20

# NOBEL PHYSICS

1. The first Nobel Laureate physicist whose offspring also received the Nobel Prize for Physics was:
   (a) Niels Bohr
   (b) Pierre Curie
   (c) Karl Siegbahn
   (d) Joseph John Thomson

2. USA leads the table of Nobel Prize winners in sciences, but she could not open her account till 22 non-American scientists received the Prize in the sciences. Who was the first American scientist to receive the Nobel Prize?
   (a) Clinton Davisson
   (b) Arthur Compton
   (c) Albert Michelson
   (d) Robert Millikan

3. A number of times the master–student pair shares the Nobel Prize in Physics. Which of the following is an exception?
   (a) Bardeen–Cooper
   (b) Bardeen–Schneider
   (c) Cockcroft–Walton
   (d) Chamberlain–Segre

4. In which of the following student–master pairs, the student received the Nobel Prize earlier than the master?
   (a) Michelson–Lippman
   (b) Fermi–Yang
   (c) Rabi–Schwinger
   (d) Heisenberg–Bohr

5. What is common to the following physicists—Arnold Sommerfeld, Henry Moseley, Paul Chu:
   (a) All these were prominent in Physics but were awarded the Nobel Prize for Chemistry.
   (b) All these have outstanding contribution in Physics, but were uncrowned Nobel Laureates.
   (c) All these were awarded the Prize when they were in their early thirties.
   (d) All these were awarded the Nobel Prize posthumously.

6. Under the tutelage of Niels Bohr, many scientists have won the Nobel Prize. Who among the following Nobel Prize winners was not his pupil?
   (a) Patrick Blackett      (b) Wolfgang Pauli
   (c) Linus Pauling      (d) Werner Heisenberg

7. Who was awarded the Nobel Prize for discovering invar, a nickel–steel alloy having very small coefficient of expansion?
   (a) Jean Bapiste Perrin
   (b) Hannes Alfven
   (c) Percy Williams Bridgman
   (d) Charles Edouard Guillaume

8. The largest chain of Nobel Prize winning teacher–student relationship extends to five decades, starting from Oswald (1909) through Glasser (1960). Which of the following statements is not correct?
   (a) Anderson studied under Millikan.
   (b) Nernst taught Millikan.
   (c) Langmuir was taught by Millikan.
   (d) Glasser was a student of Anderson.

9. The 1959 Nobel Prize was awarded to whom for demonstrating the existence of anti-proton?
   (a) Owen Chamberlain
   (b) Emilio Segre
   (c) Both Chamberlain and Segre
   (d) Carl Anderson

10. For which work Richard Feynman, Julian Schwinger, and Shinichiro Tomonaga were jointly awarded the Nobel Prize for Physics in 1965?
    (a) quantum electrodynamics
    (b) computer memories
    (c) super conductivity    (d) miniature electronics

11. The 1933 Nobel Prize for Physics was shared by two outstanding scientists for the discovery of new fertile forms of the atomic theory. One of them was Erwin Schrödinger. Who was the other?
    (a) P.M.S. Blackett        (b) P.A.M. Dirac
    (c) Otto Stern             (d) Werner Heisenberg

12. For which outstanding research two young Chinese physicists, Tsung Dao Lee and Chen Ning Yang, were awarded the Nobel Prize in 1957?
    (a) For work on energy levels inside atoms.
    (b) For determining shape and size of the atomic nucleus.
    (c) For disproving the principle of conservation of parity.
    (d) For developing cosmic ray counter.

13. A staunch supporter of Herr Hitler, he spent 4 years in a labour camp in 1947. He discovered the Doppler effect in Canal rays and the splitting of spectral lines in electric fields. Who was he, who received the Nobel Prize before Einstein?
    (a) Johannes Stark         (b) Pieter Zeeman
    (c) Guglielmo Marconi      (d) Fritz Zernike

14. He married twice. Three of his children died young. One of the two surviving sons was executed for his role in an unsuccessful attempt on the life of Herr Hitler in 1944. Engrossed in the domain of Subatomic Physics he was awarded the Nobel Prize for his discoveries in connection with the quantum theory. Who was he?
    (a) Niels Bohr        (b) Karl Siegbahn
    (c) James Franck     (d) Max Planck

15. At the age of 20, he wrote a 200-page book on the theory of relativity. At 24, he proposed the fourth quantum number. At 27, he became full-fledged professor of Physics in a university. He discovered a very important principle of Physics bearing his name. Who was this great physicist, who won the 1945 Nobel Prize for his outstanding work on atomic fissions?
    (a) Albert Einstein
    (b) Werner Heisenberg
    (c) Wolfgang Pauli
    (d) P.A.M. Dirac

16. What is common about the following Nobel Laureates—Heike Kamerlingh–Onnes, Leon Cooper, Johannes George Bednorz, John Robert Schrieffer, John Bardeen, and Karl Alex Muller. All of them were awarded the Nobel Prize for their contributions in the field of:
    (a) high energy particles    (b) transistors
    (c) superconductivity       (d) cryogenics

17. Who was awarded the Nobel Prize for the discovery of neutron?
    (a) Victor Franz Hess    (b) Sir James Chadwick
    (c) Robert Millikan       (d) Carl David Anderson

18. Three physicists shared the 1964 Nobel Prize for Physics for developing MASER and LASER principle of producing high-intensity radiation. Two of them were Nikolai Basov and Alexandr Prochorov. Who was the third?
    (a) Igor Tamm
    (b) Ilya Frank
    (c) Charles Towns
    (d) Pavel Cerenkov

19. In 1933, the Nobel Prize for 1932 was awarded to a German physicist for the creation of quantum mechanics. Who was he?
    (a) Werner Heisenberg
    (b) Max Planck
    (c) Max Born
    (d) Erwin Schrödinger

20. The existence of the massless and chargeless subatomic particle neutrino was postulated in 1931 by Wolfgang Pauli, and was first detected in 1956 by the American physicists Frederick Reines and Clyde Cowab. Name the Nobel laureate who coined the term 'neutrino'?
    (a) Isidor Isaac Rabi
    (b) Ernest Orlando Lawrence
    (c) Enrico Fermi
    (d) Otto Stern

# 21

# LITERATURE OF PHYSICS

1. Who is the Nobel Laureate author of the classic book *Radiative Transfer*?
   (a) S. Chandrasekhar          (b) William Fowler
   (c) Arno Penzias              (d) Charles Hard Townes

2. *My Development as a Physicist* is an autobiography of a Nobel Prize winning physicist, whose discovery of diffraction of X-rays in crystals is described by Albert Einstein as one of the most beautiful discoveries in Physics. Name the author of the book:
   (a) Sir William Henry Bragg
   (b) Sir William Lawrence Bragg
   (c) Max von Laue
   (d) Karl Siegbahn

3. *Interaction: A Journey Through the Mind of a Particle Physicist* is an autobiography of a leading physicist and a Nobel Prize winner as well. Who is he?
   (a) Abdus Salam
   (b) Steven Weinberg
   (c) Sheldon Glashow
   (d) James Cronin

4. Hans Bethe, who was awarded the Nobel Prize in 1967 for his work on energy production in stars, authored which of the following books?
   (a) *Physics and Beyond*
   (b) *The Road from Los Alamos*
   (c) *Breakthrough*
   (d) *The Second Creation*

5. *The Nature of Time* is based on a discussion between philosophers and physicists on the enigmatic aspect of time. Its famous author has also given a theory of the universe. Who is he?
   (a) Thomas Gold          (b) Hermann Bondi
   (c) Fred Hoyle           (d) Abbe Lamaitre

6. Which of the following books is not written by Werner Heisenberg?
   (a) *Physics and Philosophy*
   (b) *The Physical Principles of the Quantum Theory*
   (c) *Breakthrough*
   (d) *Physics and Beyond*

7. Which one of the following books is not written by Fred Hoyle?
   (a) *The Nature of the Universe*
   (b) *Survey of the Universe*
   (c) *Galaxy, Nuclei and Quasars*
   (d) *Frontiers of Astronomy*

8. *The Theory of Spectra and Atomic Constitution* is a standard book on the structure of matter. Who authored it?
   (a) S. Tolansky          (b) A. Haas
   (c) Niels Bohr           (d) G. Hertzberg

9. Max Born, the English physicist and Nobel Prize winner for Physics in 1954, is famous for his work in quantum mechanics. Two of the following books are written by him:
   I. *Einstein's Theory of Relativity*
   II. *The Universe and Dr. Einstein*
   III. *Atomic Physics*
   IV. *Space, Time and Gravitation*

   Which is the proper combination among the following?
   (a) I and III
   (b) II and IV
   (c) II and III
   (d) III and IV

10. An outstanding book on the wave nature of light titled *An Introduction to the Study of Wave Mechanics* was published in 1930. Who was its author?
    (a) P.A.M. Dirac        (b) A. Sommerfeld
    (c) E. Schroedinger     (d) Louis de Broglie

11. Two volumes of which famous book, published between 1928–1932, authored by the father–son team of J.J. Thomson and G.P. Thomson—both Nobel Prize winners in Physics:
    (a) *Conduction of Electricity through Gases*
    (b) *Electricity in Gases*
    (c) *Electrical Phenomena in Gases*
    (d) *Mobility of the Positive Ions in Gases*

12. A classic book *Matter and Light* is written by:
    (a) Werner Heisenberg      (b) J. Jeans
    (c) Louis de Broglie       (d) W. Heitler

13. Which of the following is the largest encyclopaedia of Physics?
    (a) *Handbuch der Physik*, edited by S. Flugge
    (b) *McGraw-Hill Encyclopaedia of Physics*
    (c) *Encyclopaedia of Physics* by Lerner and Trigg
    (d) *Encyclopedia of Physics* by R.M. Besançon

14. The multi-volume *Encyclopaedic Dictionary of Physics*, edited by J. Thewlis and published by Oxford Pergamon Press, has a six-language glossary of 15,000 physical terms, which includes English, French, German, Spanish and Russian. Which is the sixth language?
    (a) Arabic                  (b) Italian
    (c) Japanese                (d) Swedish

15. Which useful book on the literature of physics is written by B. Yates?
    (a) *Physics Literature*
    (b) *Use of Physics Literature*
    (c) *Guide to the Literature of Mathematics and Physics*
    (d) *How to Find Out in Physics*

16. Which of the following famous bibliographic information sources for research and developments in Physics is edited by H. Coblans?
    (a) *Current Contents*        (b) *Physics Abstracts*
    (c) *Physics Literature*
    (d) *Use of Physics Literature*

17. One of the following bibliographies written by D.F. Shaw is a standard work on the literature of Physics, and supersedes *Use of Physics Literature*. Name it:
    (a) *Information Sources in Physics*
    (b) *Reports on Progress in Physics*
    (c) *International Union of Pure and Applied Physics*
    (d) *Introductory Guide to Information Sources on Physics*

18. *A Dictionary of Named Effects and Laws in Chemistry, Physics, and Mathematics,* first published in 1976, records scientific events in chronological order. Who has written it?
    (a) J. Thewlis
    (b) D.N. Lapedes
    (c) D.W.G. Ballentyne and D.R. Lovett
    (d) C.F. Hix and R.P. Alley

19. Which of the following biographical reference books describes the most significant discoveries in Physics of the present century?
    (a) *The History of Modern Physics* by Brush and Beloni
    (b) *Nobel Prize Winners in Physics* by Heathcote
    (c) *The Biographical Dictionary of Scientists* by D. Abbot
    (d) *Literature on the History of Physics in the Twentieth Century* by Heilbron and Wheaton

20. *Dream of a Final Theory* is written by one of the most distinguished physicists of modern time, in which he imagines the shape of the final theory of all fundamental physical forces and its impact on the future of science. What is his name?
    (a) Fred Hoyle          (b) George Gamow
    (c) Steven Weinberg      (d) Stefen Hawking

# 22

# BREAKTHROUGH

1. In 1930, P.A.M. Dirac predicted the existence of anti-particles. Two years later, Carl Anderson discovered the first anti-particle—positron. In which year were anti-proton and anti-neutron discovered?
   (a) 1934                 (b) 1938
   (c) 1945                 (d) 1956

2. The first successful atom-smashing was carried out by:
   (a) Robert van de Graff
   (b) Ernest Orlando Lawrence
   (c) John Cockcroft and E.T.S. Walton
   (d) James Chadwich

3. Special theory of relativity tells that:
   I.    moving clocks run slow
   II.   moving rulers shrink
   III.  mass of moving objects increases
   (a) I only             (b) III only
   (c) I, II and III      (d) none of these

4. A semiconductor device with both active and passive electronic elements diffused into a silicon wafer to form a functional circuit is called:
   (a) hybrid circuit       (b) integrated circuit
   (c) thin-film circuit     (d) thick-film circuit

5. Name the first atomic reactor that became operational for the production of electricity in 1956:
   (a) Calder Hall, England
   (b) Shipping Port Reactor, US
   (c) The Uranium Pile, University of Chicago
   (d) 'Zoe', France

6. Ernst Ruska invented a wonderful instrument in 1934, but was awarded the Nobel Prize only in 1986 for work on it. What is his invention?
   (a) Photomultiplier
   (b) Phase contrast microscope
   (c) Electron microscope
   (d) Proton microscope

7. In which year did a group headed by Edward Teller develop the first thermonuclear device, popularly known as the Hydrogen Bomb?
   (a) 1943               (b) 1945
   (c) 1952               (d) 1954

8  In 1964, an entirely new concept of sub-atomic particles was introduced, according to which all mesons and baryons are made up of fractional charges, known as *quarks*. Which physicist introduced this concept?
   (a) Nicola Cabibbo       (b) Murry Gell-Mann
   (c) Sheldon Glashow      (d) Moo-Young Han

9. Up (u), Down (d) and Strange (s) were the three original quarks. The fourth quark was introduced in 1974 by Sheldon Glashow. What name was given to this quark?
   (a) Charm                (b) Beauty
   (c) Truth                (d) Top

10. X-ray astronomy can only be done from above the earth's atmosphere. It started with the launching of the first Small Astronomy Satellite, SAS-1, in 1970. It was designated:
    (a) Tiros                    (b) Score
    (c) Uhuru                    (d) Echo

11. The Big Bang theory of the universe was developed in 1948 by:
    (a) Georg Gamow, Hermann Bondi, and Thomas Gold.
    (b) Fred Hoyle, Robert Herman, and Thomas Gold.
    (c) Hermann Bondi, Ralf Alpher, and Georg Gamow.
    (d) Georg Gamow, Ralph Alpher, and Robert Herman.

12. The radiowave remnants of the Big Bang were accidentally discovered in 1964. Who discovered them?
    (a) Steven Weinberger and Nicola Cabibbo
    (b) Arno Penzias and Steven Weinberger
    (c) Robert Wilson and Arno Penzias
    (d) Nicola Cabibbo and Arno Penzias

13. In 1974, Burton Richter and Samuel Ting independently discovered a new sub-atomic particle that established the existence of *charm*, the fourth quark. How is this subatomic particle represented?
    (a) J                        (b) $\Psi$
    (c) J-$\Psi$                 (d) J/$\Psi$

14. Alex Müller and Georg Bednorz made a sensational discovery in 1986 when they found that a mixed oxide of lanthanum, barium, and copper turned out to be a superconductor. At what transition temperature (Tc) the ceramics prepared by them became superconducting?
    (a) 35 K                     (b) 52 K
    (c) 76 K                     (d) 93 K

15. For which outstanding discovery Antony Hewish is most famous?
    (a) quasars         (b) pulsars
    (c) masers         (d) lasers

16. The English physicist and Nobel Laureate Martin Ryle made extensive investigations using radio telescopes. What type of investigations did he make?
    (a) Probing outer space with high degree of precision.
    (b) Probing the radio stars.
    (c) Probing the organic life on the planet Mars.
    (d) Probing extra-gallactic life.

17. Who developed a theory of weak interaction that led to the electroweak theory?
    (a) Abdus Salam
    (b) Sheldon Glashow
    (c) Steven Weinberg
    (d) Nicola Cabibbo

18. Marriage between advanced Physics and Medicine is issuing novel methods to cure patients. Which of the following revolutionary techniques is used for the treatment of kidney stones?
    (a) Pion beams         (b) Jarvik 7 model
    (c) Lithotripsy         (d) Molecular beams

19. James Watson, Grancis Crick and Mauris Wilkins were awarded the 1962 Nobel Prize for Physiology for their work on DNA, the blueprint of life. Who among them was a physicist?
    (a) James Watson         (b) Francis Crick
    (c) Mauris Wilkins         (d) none of them

20. For which outstanding work was Jack Kilby awarded the 2000 Nobel Prize for Physics?
    (a) Invention of the integrated circuit.
    (b) For elucidating the quantum structure of electroweak interaction.
    (c) For development of methods to cool and trap atoms with laser light.
    (d) For the detection of the neutrino.

## 23

## END OF THE BEGINNING

1.  Einstein suggested that gravity is not really a force
    but is the result of curvature in space, and predicted
    the existence of the gravitational waves. Name the
    designer who invented the model of the gravity wave
    detector:
    (a) Robert Forward
    (b) Rochus Vogt
    (c) Joseph Weber
    (d) Rainer Weiss

2.  Name the hypothetical particles that might carry
    the grand unified forces at a temperature of $10^{28}$
    degrees?
    (a) gravitons          (b) gluons
    (c) X-bosons           (d) preons

3.  The Grand Unified Theory, GUT, which hypothesises
    the unification of electromagnetism, weak interactions
    and stong nuclear forces, predicts:
    (a) the existence of quarks of fractional electric-charge.
    (b) the existence of an 11- dimensional world.
    (c) that proton decays in $10^{31}$ years.
    (d) that neutrino has a finite rest mass.

4. According to the Grand Unified Theory, GUT, after $10^{31}$ years all the protons in the universe will fall apart, and that will be the end of the universe. When was the GUT proposed for the first time?
   (a) 1964                    (b) 1970
   (c) 1974                    (d) 1976

5. What is common to the following physicists—Jeremiah Ostriker, Kip Thorne, Joseph Taylor, and Russel Hulse?
   (a) They are in the race to detect gravitational waves.
   (b) All are associated with work on quasars.
   (c) All are working to discover tachyons, particles travelling faster than light.
   (d) They are in a race to develop superconductor working at room temperature.

6. What is LIGO?
   (a) A project to detect the gravitational wave
   (b) A project to gather signals from extra-terrestrial space
   (c) The ultimate robot
   (d) The ultimate superconductor

7. John Wheeler, one of the inventors of the hydrogen bomb, suggested the concept of Superspace, a region beyond our normal space. Following possibiliities may arise:
   I.   Many of the existing natural laws do not hold good in Superspace.
   II.  In Superspace there is neither past not future, but an endless present.
   III. Through Superspace, instantaneous travel to any part of the universe is possible.

   If you are in agreement with Prof. Wheeler, which combination is possible?
   (a) I and II only            (b) II and III only
   (c) all the above            (d) none of the above

8. What is the name of the particle accelerator, about 84 km in circumference, that can replicate the conditions prevailing in the universe some trillionth of a second after the Big Bang?
   (a) Stanford Linear Accelerator
   (b) superconducting supercollider
   (c) International Thermonuclear Experimental Reactor
   (d) Tokamak Fission Reactor

9. Paul Steinhardt, Alan Gutt, A.D. Linde, and Andreas Albrecht are associated with:
   (a) developing a Super Grand Unified Field Theory encompassing all the natural forces in one single equation.
   (b) developing a new theory of the origin of the universe.
   (c) devising a novel method to change the course of Swift Tuttle, the comet which is expected to collide with the earth in 2026.
   (d) developing a new theory of superconductivity.

10. The International Thermonuclear Experimental Reactor, ITER, sponsored by four industrial powers, is a tokamak fusion reactor. This powerful reactor was completed in the early 21st century. What does the term *tokamak* mean?
    (a) It is an acronym from Russian words that describes a thermonuclear process.
    (b) It is a Russian word meaning core of a nucleus.
    (c) It is a Russian word meaning torroidal magnetic chamber, conceived by Sakharov and Igor Tamm in the early 1950s.
    (d) It is a Russian acronym of the names of countries sponsoring the project.

11. Name the theory that suggests that elementary particles are actually tiny loops of strings and point-like structures:
    (a) GUT
    (b) Super GUT
    (c) Theory of Everything      (d) Superstring theory

12. Compton Gamma-ray Observatory not only discovered sixteen gamma-ray quasars but also completed the first ever all-sky gamma-ray survey. Where is this observatory located?
    (a) On the sea
    (b) In the orbit
    (c) In the desert of Utah
    (d) On the surface of the moon

13. Who was associated with Sheldon Glashow to write the first Grand Unified Field Theory of elementary particles?
    (a) Abdus Salam              (b) Steven Weinberger
    (c) Howard Georgi            (d) Georg Gamov

14. According to Quantum Chromodynamics, QCD, which deals with basic aspects of strong force, the quarks carry a new kind of charge that is called 'colour charge' or simply 'colours'. The 'colours' have nothing to do with the colours that we are familiar with, but like the real colours, they have similar additive properties. In QCD, the 'colours' exist in which three varieties?
    (a) red, green and blue
    (b) orange, green and blue
    (c) orange, green and violet
    (d) red, green and violet

15. The natural laws encompass an enormous range of time and space. Following statements may be of interest:
    I.  Shortest lived particles have a lifetime of about $10^{-24}$ seconds.
    II. Shortest distances that can be penetrated are about $10^{-24}$ metres.

    Which of the following combinations is true?
    (a) I only                    (b) II only
    (c) neither I or II           (d) both I and II

16. Very-long-baseline Interferometry, VLBI, is a system in which a number of radio telescopes, thousands of kilometres apart are linked together to gather information from distant galaxies. What is its objective?
    (a) Direct determination of the Hubble constant.
    (b) Estimation of the limits of the universe.
    (c) Finding the possiblities of intelligent life in far galaxies.
    (d) Estimation of sizes of various galaxies.

17. Which famous cosmologist authored *Is the End in Sight for Theoretical Physics*?
    (a) Gerardt Hooft             (b) Stephen Hawking
    (c) Joel Scherk               (d) Yoichirfo Nambu

18. Physicists visualise the hidden dimensions of space and time. Some think of 11-D world, the others hypothesise a 26-D space-time. But who was the physicist who first proposed the idea of space-time dimensions beyond four?
    (a) Joel Scherk               (b) John Schwarz
    (c) Theodor Kaluza            (d) Oskar Klein

19. A type of Unified Field Theory, GUT, in which the theory of relativity is extended to more than four dimensions is known as:
    (a) Hlavaty–Einstein theory
    (b) Kaluza–Klein theory
    (c) Wheeler–Misner theory
    (d) Weyl theorv

20. Gerd Binnig and Heinrich Rohrer shared the 1986 Nobel Prize with Ernst Ruska. For which work is Ruska most famous?
    (a) For the design of the first electron microscope
    (b) For the design of the scanning tunnelling microscope
    (c) For the development of high-resolution electron spectroscopy
    (d) For the development of the holographic method

# 24

# MISCELLANY

1. A grave in Stadtfriedhof belonging to one of the most brilliant minds of modern age, bears the relation $h = 6.62 \times 10^{-27}$ erg-sec at its foot. Who was this great physicist?
   (a) Paul Apstein
   (b) Erwin Schrödinger
   (c) Max Planck
   (d) Werner Heisenberg

2. A sixteen-line verse entitled *Electric Valentine* was published anonymously in the issue of *Nature* dated 30 May 1872. It was later discovered that it was written by a famous physicist. Who was he?
   (a) Humphry Davy
   (b) James Clerk Maxwell
   (c) William Rankine
   (d) William Thomson

3. John Pierce is an expert in electronics, and a famous science fiction writer. He writes under the pseudonym:
   (a) J.J. Coupling       (b) electron
   (c) J/Ψ                 (d) Isaac Asimov

4. Sometimes, scientists acquire a university degree in one discipline and learn another themselves. Before becoming an astronomer, Ejnar Hertrzsprung, famous for his H-R diagram—a method for correlating stellar data—was a:
   (a) medical practitioner     (b) theologist
   (c) chemical engineer        (d) biologist

5. Sometimes, ego reigns supreme among celebrated scientists. Sir Isaac Newton was reluctant to accept the presidency of the famous Royal Society, until one of the members was no longer associated with the Royal Society. Who was 'this' famous scientist Newton was mentioning?
   (a) Robert Hooke             (b) Francis Bacon
   (c) James Gregory            (d) Christopher Wren

6. If the height of a man is 1 unit, the diameter of our galaxy is:
   (a) $10^{10}$                (b) $10^{20}$
   (c) $10^{30}$                (d) $10^{40}$

7. Commonly, it is said that there is a conflict between science and religion, but many men of science are actively associated with religion. Who among the following astronomers was also a Polish bishop?
   (a) Charles Messier          (b) Grote Reber
   (c) Nicolaus Copernicus      (d) Ernst Öpik

8. Which physicist in 1972 filed a suit against Emilio Segre and Owen Chamberlain, charging that the design of a 1955 experiment, for which they were awarded the 1959 Nobel Prize for Physics was his idea?
   (a) Ernst Mach               (b) Lise Meitner
   (c) Willem de Sitter         (d) Oreste Piccioni

9. From spacelab research, it was found that in the absence of gravity:
   I. muscles may deteriorate.
   II. human immune system may alter.
   III. bones may become smaller and weaker.

   Which combination is correct?
   (a) I and II        (b) I and III
   (c) II and III       (d) I, II and III

10. What are the following—Lapis Lazuli, Peridot, Spinel, Tourmaline?
    (a) gem materials      (b) names of stars
    (c) asteroids         (d) moon's craters

11. One of the products of the special theory of relativity was the famous mass–energy relation: $E = mc^2$. Who, in 1900, proposed the formula on general grounds?
    (a) Herman Minkowski    (b) Arthur Eddington
    (c) Satyendra Nath Bose   (d) Henri Poincaré

12. Quarks are supposed to be the ultimate fundamental particles, but to Abdus Salam, first and only Nobel Laureate from Pakistan, a quark is also made up of even smaller particles which he calls:
    (a) SUSY particles     (b) sleptons
    (c) preons           (d) squarks

13. The time–scale ratio of light crossing a proton to Hubble time-scale is about $10^{-40}$, which, incidentally is also the ratio of the gravitational force to the electric force. This 'correspondence' led which physicist to hypothesise, in 1937 that this should be accepted as one of the laws of nature?
    (a) S. Chandrasekhar    (b) Paul Dirac
    (c) Werner Heisenberg    (d) Max Planck

14. Murry Gell-Mann won the Nobel Prize in 1969 for his outstanding work on quarks and the 'eight-fold' way. The 'eight-fold' that he coined to explain a particle classification system was named after:
    (a) realising the correspondence between Particle Physics and Eastern Mysticism.
    (b) Chinese concept of yin (broken line) and yang (solid line) to form 'eight trigrams', which in Chinese philosophy are considered to represent all possible cosmic and human situations.
    (c) the Buddhist path of enlightenment.
    (d) the hypothetical concept of eight-dimensional universe.

15. It is believed that the earth along with the rest of the solar system was formed 4.5 billion years ago. The age is determined by:
    (a) dendrocronology
    (b) fission-track dating
    (c) dating radioactive isotopes in meteorites
    (d) racemisation

16. Big Bang took place some 20 billion years ago. Particles started to be created at $10^{-43}$ seconds after the Big Bang. This extremely small time in the cosmic time-scale is known as:
    (a) Planck time
    (b) quark time
    (c) gluon time
    (d) singularity

17. From the Spacelab Biorack experiments to study the effects of micro-gravity on the development of life from embryonic stage to adulthood on fruit flies, it was observed that micro-gravity:
    I. helps increase the number of eggs.
    II. reduces the life-span of the male flies.
    III. increases the life-span of the female flies.
    IV. reduces the rate of development of eggs.

    Which of the following combination is correct?
    (a) I, II and III            (b) I, II and IV
    (c) II, III and IV           (d) I, III and IV

18. Samuel C.C. Ting, who shared the Nobel Prize in 1976 with Burton Richter, discovered a particle which he called 'J' (Richter called it Ψ). What does 'J' signify?
    (a) The character 'J' in some Chinese dialects is pronounced 'Ting'.
    (b) First letter of Jeremiah, a prophet who urged the Jewish people to moral reforms.
    (c) The symbol 'J' connotes energy-unit.
    (d) The letter of 'Jung' (Carl Gustave), the famous psychoanalyst who proposed the existence of collective unconscious.

19. Quark, the ultimate fundamental particle, is a German slang meaning *nonsense*, as well as a German word for a type of dessert. It was used in Physics by Murry Gell-Mann, but who coined it?
    (a) Johann Wolfgang von Goethe in his book *The Sorrows of Young Werther*.
    (b) The German novelist Erich Kästner in his *Emil and the Detectives*.
    (c) James Joyce in *Finnegans Wake*.
    (d) Austrian novelist Franz Werfel in *Between Heaven and Earth*.

20. The father of the Russian hydrogen bomb, Andrei Sakharov, in 1950 suggested to heat up plasma (the fourth state of matter) by inserting it in a doughnut-shaped chamber under the action of horizontal and vertical magnetic fields. This toroidal chamber is called:
   (a) Teplokhod
   (b) Tokamak
   (c) Minatura Atom
   (d) Utute Tort

**25**

# NEW PHYSICS

1. This carrier of inter-quark force plays the same role in quantum chromodynamics (QCD) as photon in quantum electrodynamics (QED). What is its name?
   (a) Higgs particle          (b) Gluon
   (c) X-boson                 (d) Higgsino

2. Gluons carry 'colour' charges. When a gluon is emitted, the 'colour' of the quark changes. How many different types of gluons are there?
   (a) 2                       (b) 4
   (c) 6                       (d) 8

3. Baryon number is a quantity assigned to elementary particles. Quarks and anti-quarks are assigned 1/3 and –1/3. Which of the following particles has baryon number zero?
   (a) Electron                (b) Proton
   (c) Neutron                 (d) Mu-meson

4. Name the fundamental particle of all hadrons:
   (a) Wino                    (b) Zino
   (c) Quark                   (d) Squark

5. Name the hypothetical particle, predicted by Grand Unification Theories (GUTs), that is able to change a quark into an qnti-quark or a lepton:
   (a) W-particle  (b) X-particle
   (c) Z-particle  (d) Higgs particle

6. It has been found that though nuclear forces and electromagnetic forces are entirely different, they are controlled by the same principle. What is this principle called?
   (a) Gauge transformation  (b) Gauge symmetry
   (c) Gauge invariance  (d) Gauge groupe

7. According to some Grand Unification Theories (GUTs) some objects have extremely small thickness ($10^{-31}$ m) and as massive as $10^7$ solar masses per light year, and play a crucial role in the formation of galactic structures. What are these objects called?
   (a) Cooper pair  (b) Rydberg atom
   (c) Super strings  (d) Cosmic strings

8. Name the radiation having a temperature of about 3 K that is supposed to be uniformly distributed in the universe:
   (a) Hawking radiation
   (b) Microwave background radiation
   (c) Cosmic radiation
   (d) Gravitational radiation

9. The generalisation of Euclidean geometry that describes an irregular or fragmented pattern, and finds application in chaos theory, is known as:
   (a) fractal geometry  (b) gauge symmetry
   (c) topology  (d) light cone

10. Name the latest theory of Fundamental Physics in which the basic entity is a one-dimensional object as against the 'zero-dimensional' points representing the elementary particles:
    (a) symmetry
    (b) supersymmetry
    (c) string theory
    (d) superstring theory

11. A magnetic monopole is believed to act as a source of radial magnetic field lines. P.A.M. Dirac was the first to realise its existence. Which pair of the following physicists seriously worked out to frame a model for the existence of a magnetic monopole?
    (a) Jogesh Pati and Abdus Salam
    (b) John Illiopoulous and D.J. Thouless
    (c) Claude Bouchiat and Philip Meyer
    (d) 't Hooft and Polyakov

12. Drell–Yan process concerns the annihilation of a quark and an anti-quark which produces:
    (a) X-particles
    (b) leptons
    (c) W and Z bosons
    (d) tau leptons

13. Predicted to exist by some GUTs, the false vacuum is the driving force behind the rapid expansion in the inflationary universe model. Which of the following is not correct about false vacuum?
    (a) It has no structure.
    (b) It has been detected by Weber bar.
    (c) Motion through it cannot be detected.
    (d) It has a large energy density and a large negative pressure.

14. Which theory involves the idea of multidimensional spaces—10 dimensions for fermions and 26 dimensions for bosons?
    (a) supergravity
    (b) string theory
    (c) superstring theory
    (d) superspace theory

15. What are zino, wino, gluino, and photino?
    (a) The fermion partners of bosons
    (b) The boson partners of fermions
    (c) The leptonic partners of hadrons
    (d) The hadronic partners of leptons

16. What are selectron, squark, and slepton?
    (a) The fermion partners of bosons
    (b) The boson partners of fermions
    (c) The leptonic partners of hadrons
    (d) The hadronic partners of leptons

17. Name the hypothetical particle having zero spin and non-zero mass that is predicted to exist by certain gauge theories:
    (a) Boson                    (b) Gauge boson
    (c) Higgs boson              (d) Zwitterion

18. This particle is the photon of the electromagnetic interaction, the gluon of the strong interaction, the W and Z particles of the weak interaction, and the graviton of the gravitational interaction. Name the particle:
    (a) Gauge boson              (b) Higgs boson
    (c) Xi-particle              (d) Upsilon particle

19. Who is the odd one out in announcing the four laws of black hole mechanics?
    (a) Brandon Carton           (b) Roy Kerr
    (c) Stephen Hawking          (d) James Bardeen

20. An essential component of GUTs is the phenomenon of spontaneous symmetry breaking, which is induced by a set of fundamental fields known as:
    (a) Virtual field            (b) Gauge field
    (c) Higgs field              (d) Group field

# ANSWERS

1. PHYSICS IN THE PAST

| | | | | |
|---|---|---|---|---|
| 1(d) | 2(c) | 3(b) | 4(b) | 5(c) |
| 6(a) | 7(b) | 8(c) | 9(a) | 10(d) |
| 11(c) | 12(c) | 13(b) | 14(d) | 15(c) |
| 16(c) | 17(b) | 18(d) | 19(b) | 20(a) |

2. CONTEMPLATION OF IDEAS

| | | | | |
|---|---|---|---|---|
| 1(a) | 2(b) | 3(c) | 4(a) | 5(d) |
| 6(b) | 7(c) | 8(b) | 9(d) | 10(a) |
| 11(b) | 12(d) | 13(b) | 14(a) | 15(a) |
| 16(c) | 17(b) | 18(c) | 19(a) | 20(b) |

3. MEASUREMENT AND PHYSICAL UNITS

| | | | | |
|---|---|---|---|---|
| 1(a) | 2(c) | 3(b) | 4(d) | 5(d) |
| 6(b) | 7(a) | 8(c) | 9(a) | 10(a) |
| 11(d) | 12(c) | 13(b) | 14(b) | 15(c) |
| 16(b) | 17(d) | 18(a) | 19(c) | 20(c) |

4. FROM ALPHA TO OMEGA

| | | | | |
|---|---|---|---|---|
| 1(c) | 2(d) | 3(c) | 4(c) | 5(a) |
| 6(c) | 7(b) | 8(c) | 9(b) | 10(d) |
| 11(b) | 12(c) | 13(d) | 14(a) | 15(a) |
| 16(a) | 17(c) | 18(b) | 19(b) | 20(d) |

5. CLASSICAL MECHANICS

| | | | | |
|---|---|---|---|---|
| 1(b) | 2(c) | 3(a) | 4(d) | 5(d) |
| 6(a) | 7(c) | 8(b) | 9(d) | 10(d) |
| 11(b) | 12(d) | 13(a) | 14(b) | 15(d) |
| 16(c) | 17(c) | 18(d) | 19(b) | 20(c) |

## 6. DOMAIN OF THE FORCES

| | | | | |
|---|---|---|---|---|
| 1(b) | 2(d) | 3(c) | 4(a) | 5(b) |
| 6(d) | 7(b) | 8(b) | 9(b) | 10(b) |
| 11(c) | 12(d) | 13(c) | 14(a) | 15(b) |
| 16(a) | 17(d) | 18(c) | 19(b) | 20(a) |

## 7. ENERGY SCENARIO

| | | | | |
|---|---|---|---|---|
| 1(b) | 2(d) | 3(c) | 4(a) | 5(d) |
| 6(c) | 7(b) | 8(b) | 9(d) | 10(c) |
| 11(a) | 12(c) | 13(b) | 14(d) | 15(a) |
| 16(c) | 17(d) | 18(a) | 19(b) | 20(b) |

## 8. CAUSE AND EFFECT

| | | | | |
|---|---|---|---|---|
| 1(b) | 2(c) | 3(a) | 4(a) | 5(d) |
| 6(c) | 7(a) | 8(c) | 9(a) | 10(b) |
| 11(d) | 12(c) | 13(a) | 14(a) | 15(b) |
| 16(c) | 17(d) | 18(a) | 19(c) | 20(a) |

## 9. IDEAS IN ACTION

| | | | | |
|---|---|---|---|---|
| 1(a) | 2(c) | 3(c) | 4(b) | 5(a) |
| 6(b) | 7(c) | 8(a) | 9(b) | 10(a) |
| 11(c) | 12(a) | 13(b) | 14(d) | 15(d) |
| 16(c) | 17(d) | 18(b) | 19(a) | 20(d) |

## 10. PHYSICAL PHENOMENA

| | | | | |
|---|---|---|---|---|
| 1(c) | 2(c) | 3(a) | 4(b) | 5(c) |
| 6(d) | 7(a) | 8(b) | 9(c) | 10(d) |
| 11(c) | 12(d) | 13(b) | 14(c) | 15(a) |
| 16(b) | 17(a) | 18(c) | 19(b) | 20(d) |

## 11. KITH AND KIN OF PHYSICS

| | | | | |
|---|---|---|---|---|
| 1(b) | 2(d) | 3(a) | 4(a) | 5(b) |
| 6(d) | 7(d) | 8(c) | 9(b) | 10(c) |
| 11(a) | 12(d) | 13(b) | 14(d) | 15(a) |
| 16(d) | 17(d) | 18(a) | 19(b) | 20(a) |

## 12. VIBRANT PHYSICS

| | | | | |
|---|---|---|---|---|
| 1(a) | 2(d) | 3(c) | 4(a) | 5(d) |
| 6(c) | 7(b) | 8(a) | 9(c) | 10(c) |
| 11(d) | 12(c) | 13(d) | 14(c) | 15(b) |
| 16(c) | 17(b) | 18(a) | 19(c) | 20(c) |

## 13. MATERIAL PROPERTIES

| | | | | |
|---|---|---|---|---|
| 1(c) | 2(a) | 3(c) | 4(a) | 5(d) |
| 6(c) | 7(c) | 8(b) | 9(a) | 10(c) |
| 11(a) | 12(b) | 13(a) | 14(c) | 15(b) |
| 16(b) | 17(a) | 18(a) | 19(d) | 20(c) |

## 14. MICROCOSMOS

| | | | | |
|---|---|---|---|---|
| 1(c) | 2(c) | 3(d) | 4(b) | 5(b) |
| 6(a) | 7(c) | 8(b) | 9(a) | 10(b) |
| 11(d) | 12(d) | 13(b) | 14(d) | 15(a) |
| 16(b) | 17(c) | 18(b) | 19(d) | 20(d) |

## 15. MACROCOSMOS

| | | | | |
|---|---|---|---|---|
| 1(d) | 2(b) | 3(c) | 4(c) | 5(b) |
| 6(c) | 7(a) | 8(d) | 9(c) | 10(b) |
| 11(d) | 12(a) | 13(b) | 14(c) | 15(a) |
| 16(d) | 17(b) | 18(c) | 19(b) | 20(a) |

## 16. LOGICAL PHYSICS

| | | | | |
|---|---|---|---|---|
| 1(a) | 2(d) | 3(a) | 4(d) | 5(a) |
| 6(d) | 7(b) | 8(a) | 9(b) | 10(c) |
| 11(b) | 12(a) | 13(d) | 14(a) | 15(d) |
| 16(a) | 17(c) | 18(b) | 19(c) | 20(d) |

## 17. MAKERS OF PHYSICS

| | | | | |
|---|---|---|---|---|
| 1(a) | 2(c) | 3(a) | 4(c) | 5(d) |
| 6(b) | 7(c) | 8(d) | 9(a) | 10(a) |
| 11(b) | 12(c) | 13(d) | 14(b) | 15(d) |
| 16(c) | 17(b) | 18(d) | 19(c) | 20(a) |

## 18. REASONING IN PHYSICS

| | | | | |
|---|---|---|---|---|
| 1(d) | 2(a) | 3(d) | 4(c) | 5(c) |
| 6(d) | 7(a) | 8(c) | 9(b) | 10(a) |
| 11(c) | 12(d) | 13(b) | 14(c) | 15(b) |
| 16(c) | 17(a) | 18(a) | 19(b) | 20(c) |

## 19. EXPERIMENTAL PHYSICS

| | | | | |
|---|---|---|---|---|
| 1(d) | 2(b) | 3(a) | 4(b) | 5(a) |
| 6(b) | 7(d) | 8(a) | 9(b) | 10(d) |
| 11(a) | 12(d) | 13(b) | 14(a) | 15(b) |
| 16(c) | 17(b) | 18(c) | 19(a) | 20(c) |

## 20. NOBEL PHYSICS

| | | | | |
|---|---|---|---|---|
| 1(d) | 2(c) | 3(c) | 4(a) | 5(b) |
| 6(a) | 7(d) | 8(c) | 9(c) | 10(a) |
| 11(b) | 12(c) | 13(a) | 14(d) | 15(c) |
| 16(c) | 17(b) | 18(c) | 19(a) | 20(c) |

## 21. LITERATURE OF PHYSICS

| | | | | |
|---|---|---|---|---|
| 1(a) | 2(c) | 3(c) | 4(b) | 5(a) |
| 6(c) | 7(b) | 8(c) | 9(a) | 10(d) |
| 11(a) | 12(c) | 13(a) | 14(c) | 15(d) |
| 16(d) | 17(a) | 18(c) | 19(b) | 20(c) |

## 22. BREAKTHROUGH

| | | | | |
|---|---|---|---|---|
| 1(d) | 2(c) | 3(d) | 4(b) | 5(a) |
| 6(c) | 7(c) | 8(b) | 9(a) | 10(c) |
| 11(d) | 12(c) | 13(d) | 14(a) | 15(b) |
| 16(a) | 17(d) | 18(c) | 19(b) | 20(a) |

## 23. THE END OF THE BEGINNING

| | | | | |
|---|---|---|---|---|
| 1(c) | 2(c) | 3(d) | 4(b) | 5(a) |
| 6(a) | 7(c) | 8(b) | 9(b) | 10(c) |
| 11(d) | 12(b) | 13(c) | 14(a) | 15(d) |
| 16(a) | 17(b) | 18(c) | 19(b) | 20(a) |

## 24. MISCELLANY

| | | | | |
|---|---|---|---|---|
| 1(c) | 2(b) | 3(a) | 4(c) | 5(a) |
| 6(b) | 7(c) | 8(d) | 9(d) | 10(a) |
| 11(d) | 12(c) | 13(b) | 14(c) | 15(c) |
| 16(a) | 17(b) | 18(a) | 19(c) | 20(b) |

## 25. NEW PHYSICS

| | | | | |
|---|---|---|---|---|
| 1(b) | 2(d) | 3(a) | 4(c) | 5(b) |
| 6(c) | 7(d) | 8(b) | 9(a) | 10(c) |
| 11(d) | 12(a) | 13(b) | 14(c) | 15(a) |
| 16(b) | 17(c) | 18(a) | 19(b) | 20(c) |